THE ENTREPRENEUR ENIGMA

A WEAL & WOE BOOKSHOP WITCH MYSTERY

CATE MARTIN

Cover design by Shezaad Sudar.

Ratatoskr Press logo by Aidan Vincent Kise.

ISBN 978-1-958606-70-4

❀ Created with Vellum

I had only been working in the Weal & Woe Bookshop for three months, but somehow even in that short span of time, it had become the center of my entire world.

I mean, I had always loved books. And libraries and bookshops had always been my sanctuaries wherever I had found them. Every new school I was transferred to after only spending a few weeks at the last one, they all had libraries filled with books that felt familiar, even if many of them were new to me. If I needed a safe place to be alone after yet another humiliating inability to do a simple magic spell in some class or other, those libraries were always there. And the books were my comfort when I had no friends. Books were my support and guidance in the times when my mother, my only known family member, felt so impossibly far away.

But those days were over. I wasn't in school anymore. And since moving to the Square—a magical neighborhood in the St. Anthony area of Minneapolis just a stone's throw from the Mississippi River— I had made actual friends. Like, real human people that I saw more than once a day.

And I had found a family, first an uncle I had not remembered until I met him again, and then a brother I had never known of at all. My mother was still a distant phantom who flitted in and out of my life for all too brief moments until even that had stopped a few months before, but she wasn't everything to me anymore. She was just a mother now.

So you'd think, given all that, that the center of my world would be the Square itself. My best friend Audrey owned the teashop where I had breakfast every single day. My boyfriend Steph lived in the magically transported European castle tower that dominated an entire corner of the Square, and I spent a ton of time with him there learning all about the particular brand of magic that I had never even known I had until I'd come to the Square.

And I had other friends as well. Cressida, the woman who helped me get the frazzled mass of my hair under control, was one. Barnardo, the man who joined my best friend and me for tea and scones every morning so he could share the latest gossip with us, was another. And I was quickly forming another friendship with Violenta, the woman who ran the boutique and was putting a lot more thought into my perfect fall and winter wardrobe than I'd ever put into anything clothes-related, ever.

It was weird, having so many people who just cared about me.

But as much as I loved the Square and nearly everyone in it, it was still the Weal & Woe Bookshop that was the focal point of my life. The building itself had nurtured me since I'd come to watch the place so my uncles could take a long-delayed honeymoon trip to Europe. The bookshop adjusted its lighting and temperature for my comfort the minute I stepped inside. It had created an entire cozy little nook for me to do research in, or just curl up with a book and pass a few quiet hours.

It felt like home in a way no place else ever had. Which I guess isn't too surprising, coming from a kid who had grown up in boarding schools, and a lot of different boarding schools at that. Boarding schools that looked after me over the holidays as well. Year-round I lived in dorms, but never for more than a few weeks in one place. Of course, the one place I had lived in for almost four months was going to feel special.

But my uncles were on their way home now. They were coming back in the morning through the magical portal that stood in the heart of the hedge maze in the open space that was too big to be called a mere courtyard in the center of the Square.

They were coming back, and then they would take over the running of their shop again, too. Because of course they would.

But I'd been there long enough to know the shop didn't really need both of them working there. There definitely wasn't a need for a third person.

There wasn't a need for me.

I knew my uncles weren't going to throw me out, of course. I just didn't know what *was* going to happen. What was I going to do next?

Every time I started to try to ask, my throat would dry up, choking away the words before I could utter them. I would disconnect the call without asking my uncle Carlo anything at all.

And every time I thought about what kind of plans I might make, my brain would dry up and choke as well. And my heart would start pounding, and my palms would start sweating, and it would get so hard to breathe that I would get lightheaded.

It wasn't a good feeling.

So I ended up spending more and more time inside the bookshop, and especially inside my little nook. Like I was trying to soak up all the warm feelings of the place in case I wasn't going to need to have access to the memories of those feelings in the future. Which was silly. Even if I didn't work there, my uncles wouldn't mind if I just hung out there reading books. I was *sure* that was true.

But still. The night before they were due back, I was there again, long past midnight, lurking in my nook.

I had gone down to the bookshop after dinner with the idea that I should make sure everything was shipshape before their return in the morning. Only I had never done anything to make it not shipshape. Everything was just as it should be. All the deliveries had been unboxed and shelved. The inventory in the computer was up to date. Every inquiry that had appeared on the pages of the magic tome that connected the Weal & Woe Bookshop with every other magical bookshop in the world had been read and responded to.

I had even dusted the shelves. Which was saying something. The Weal & Woe Bookshop was seven massive floors, each floor jammed with shelf after shelf of books, as well as racks of tightly rolled scrolls, tables of artifacts and magical instruments of which I could name only a few, and desks for visitors to linger and work at like the bookshop was a library. Which, for some, it kind of was.

That was a lot of dusting. And not a bit of it had been necessary. The magic of the Weal & Woe Bookshop just kept the interior dust-free all on its own. I had just wanted to take the time to see everything. In case I was saying goodbye.

So after shutting down the shop computer for the second time that day, I had wandered up to the fourth floor, to where my nook lay centered around a window that overlooked the prosaic Minneapolis street just outside the reach of the spells that protected the Square.

My companion followed close at my heels, not saying a word, which was a little unusual for him. Houdini looked like a black rat terrier-chihuahua, a dog so little at under ten pounds that most cats were larger than him, not that he ever let that intimidate him in the least.

I say he *looked* like a rat terrier-chihuahua because that was only a disguise, an illusion created by a wizard named Agatha Mirken. Her magic had been so powerful that even now, after she was dead, only the strongest of wizards would look at Houdini twice, and even they would only know something was off. They would never guess the truth.

Which was that Houdini wasn't a dog at all. He was a baby dragon. And he could talk, speaking in a deep voice in the back of my mind, or the minds of others if he so chose.

And talk he did, sometimes a bit too much, if I'm being honest.

But that night he was unusually quiet. At first I just thought he was reading my mood. That he sensed my need for quiet self-reflection.

But then we reached my little nook and from the dim light from the street lamps far below, I saw that we were not alone inside the bookshop.

My newfound brother Mercutio was there, standing with his back to me, his hands in his pockets as he gazed out that window. I guessed the shop had dimmed the lights to assist him in seeing whatever he was looking at outside, but at my approach, they slowly brightened to a more comfortable reading level. Now I could make out the details of his carefully selected prosaic outfit, ordinary jeans and a T-shirt with canvas sneakers that were just starting to show signs of wear.

Not that he stood much chance of blending in with any crowd. He might be dressed like one of the prosaics he was currently living among, but he had gotten all of our mother's breathtaking good looks. And he still wore his raven-black hair long and loose, falling nearly to his hips. That, with his pale skin, always made it look like he'd just be more comfortable cosplaying as a vampire from a movie or something. He belonged in dark colors and Edwardian ruffles.

"Mercutio," I said, even as I bent to pick Houdini up. Now Houdini's silence made sense. I might not have known I even had a brother until a month ago, but I had spent at least breakfast time with him every day since, and more than a few afternoons or evenings catching up with him. He had never shown a single sign that I couldn't trust him.

And yet it still felt safer, not letting him in on Houdini's secret.

And as much as I knew he'd only ever been a middling student in his academy days, he had still been studying to be a ritual magician. Very few even made it into those programs, and none of those who did were to be underestimated.

It was safer for Houdini not to talk around Mercutio, even though we were pretty sure no one could hear Houdini unless he wanted them to.

Pretty sure wasn't sure enough. Dragons were rare in our world. Rare, but powerful. And what wasn't rare in our world were wizards willing to do anything to get their hands on that kind of power. Just the thought of Houdini bound against his will to some nefarious sorcerer sent a cold chill up my spine.

Not that I thought Mercutio would try to snare a dragon. But he might let some word slip to someone who would.

Better safe than sorry. Better Houdini continue pretending to be a mere dog.

At the sound of his name, Mercutio turned away from the window and gave me a smile. "Sorry to stop by so late," he said.

"Why didn't you come up to the apartment?" I asked.

"I figured you'd be here," he said with a shrug. "How are you doing? Are you getting nervous?"

"Why would I be nervous?" I asked. Which, especially paired with the way I chewed at my lip while waiting for his answer, was definitely not a denial that I was nervous.

"I know how much this place means to you," he said. "Not that you've ever said so, not in so many words. But I could tell you loved being in charge here. And now you won't be, after tomorrow morning. It must be tough."

"I guess," I said. Houdini batted at my chin with his paw, so I cuddled him closer and nuzzled the top of his head. As always, I was careful not to touch his ears. He was sensitive about those cute little radar dishes.

"Hey, I know if you need to talk to someone about it, you're probably going to talk to your best friend Audrey or your boyfriend Steph," he said. He stumbled just a little over that last name. The two of them—both ritual magicians by training and therefore still feeling the encouragement of their schooldays to view each other as bitter competitors—had been cordial enough with each other, but I didn't think they'd ever actually be friends.

But he went on, "I'm just saying, having recently had my entire future derail on me, I know what it feels like. Not that I think you're about to have your life derailed or anything!" he quickly corrected himself, even taking his hands out of his pockets to wave them around in desperate denial.

"What's going on, Mercutio?" I asked him. Houdini made a little growly noise, like he had an answer that he really wanted to give me. As much as he was choosing not to speak, he was listening in as attentively as ever.

"I just thought..." he said, then broke off with a sigh that seemed to deflate his entire body. "I don't know. I know we missed a whole childhood together, so this relationship now is not what it should be. And I don't want you to feel like I'm trying to force you into more closeness than you actually feel. I just thought, well, I've kind of been where you are. I mean, there was one night in particular, after my last application had gone off to the last apprenticeship that would even consider me. And I remember not sleeping at all that night. And here *you* are. So I just thought, maybe we could relate?"

He was radiating anxiety. I was pretty sure if he had a way to teleport away in a blink like Steph could, he would totally be doing it right now. But without that particular skill, he was stuck where he was, waiting for my answer.

"I didn't know you felt that way," I said. "We've been hanging out a lot. Like, every day."

Hanging out, and chatting about random topics like current events in the magical or prosaics worlds, or memories from our school days. But anytime I tried to bring up anything more personal, like about our mother or rarer still the father I didn't know at all, he would always change the subject. Or make an excuse and leave.

He hadn't told me one new thing about our family or our past since moving here from Chicago. Even though he promised he would.

"I know, I know," he said. "It's been great. You've been great."

But he was chewing his lip now. Just like I always did when I wanted to melt into the ground and disappear.

And I remembered we had the same smile, too. We shared a lot. We just didn't share any memories.

But he was finally trying. This olive branch he was trying to extend to me was at least a personal one. It didn't involve any details about our parents, but it was about him, personally. It was a start.

"Hey," I said, walking closer to him despite Houdini's rumble of protest, so low I felt it against my chest more than I heard it. I patted Mercutio's arm a bit awkwardly.

He might have gotten his looks from our mother, but the muscle in that arm had been all his own doing. There was no reason I knew of for a ritual magician to be built like a hockey player.

Or, perhaps more accurately, a martial artist.

I still had so many questions about him.

"Look, it's late," I said. "I appreciate what you're saying, and you're totally right. I can see where you can relate to me in a way the others just can't. But right now, I'm just trying to settle my own mind. And I kind of have to do that on my own."

"Sure," he said, nodding in a way that made me suspect his chief emotion in that moment was relief. Like coming to see if I needed him had been checking an obligation box, one he was happy hadn't led to more boxes.

Weird. I still didn't get him. At all.

"They are coming in at dawn. Did you want to be there to meet them? I know Uncle Carlo is looking forward to meeting you. I've told him all about you," I said.

"No, that's not the right time," he said. "Definitely later, I want to meet him for sure. But that first moment back, that's too soon. And anyway, I don't want to distract from your happy reunion."

"I've only known him for four months, and for most of those, we've only been chatting on the phone," I told him.

"Still, family is family," Mercutio said.

"We're all family," I reminded him.

"I know. Trust me, that isn't the right time for me to see him," he said.

But I knew that look in his eyes, the eyes that were the same eerily beautiful shade of blue as our mother's. I had seen it a few times before during the last month. It meant that no matter how much I pushed, he wasn't going to explain himself.

It was annoying, but I had learned to respect it. Because if I tried pushing anyway, his temper would go south into grumpy territory in a hurry. And I was trying to bond with the guy, not find reasons not to like my own brother.

So I backed off. Again.

"I'll see you at breakfast, though, right?" he asked, his tone light again. "You can tell me how it all went."

"Sure," I agreed, and summoned up a smile.

He returned it, then hustled back down the steps and out into the street below.

He seemed to prefer the prosaic world, now that he was out in it. The inside of the teashop and the nook inside the bookshop were as far into the Square as he went these days, and that felt deliberate.

Maybe that was why he didn't want to meet my uncles when they returned at dawn. The portal was at the very center of the Square.

Or maybe it was just awkwardness. My uncle had known no more about Mercutio than I had when my brother had suddenly popped into my life the month before. Carlo had thought I was an only child, just as I always had. Neither of us knew what to make of the huge secret my mother had kept from both of us.

And neither of us knew why she had kept it.

Although I was working on some theories.

CHAPTER

TWO

I stood alone for a moment, looking around my nook. The long, heavy wooden table was covered, as always, in stacks of books and scrolls. The current mix was half books about the history, biology, and sociology of dragons and half research into magical astronomy.

The first was for Houdini, of course. As much as we knew for a fact he had been born a dragon, he had just been hatched when Agatha had transformed him into a dog, and no one had been able to work out yet which sort of dragon he was, let alone who his family might be.

If Agatha herself had ever known, she hadn't told anyone before her untimely end. Not even Houdini.

But the second bunch of books was my really desperate bit of wishful researching. The month before, Steph and I had gotten close to getting our hands on a book that might have explained a little about my own hereditary branch of magic, the forbidden magic of chaos. But before we'd been able to so much as glance at the cover, the man who had brought it to us had decided instead to set it and himself on fire.

I didn't like revisiting that memory. The smell, the sound, all of it had been pure horror.

All I knew about the text was that it had been tucked away inside of a book about binary systems of stars. And as much as Steph kept assuring me the two had nothing in common besides the connections an insane wizard had once made, it was all I had to go on. Maybe astronomy had something to teach me about myself.

A month of reading had yet to turn up anything, except for the sure knowledge that the math involved in really understanding these things was beyond me. Which explained the sudden appearance of calculus books at the end of the table. The bookshop had known before I had that I would soon give in to the inevitable impulse to understand something new, as daunting as that educational process was doomed to be.

Whatever Mercutio had thought of those titles—if he'd even perused them—he hadn't given any hint of it. But I should probably be a little more careful about putting things away when I wasn't using them.

I was still caught in that reverie when I heard the words, "I was starting to think he'd never leave."

"He was here for barely five minutes," I said as I put Houdini down on the ground.

"What? I didn't say anything," Houdini grumbled at me as he climbed into his favorite chair at the head of the table.

Those words hadn't been his voice inside my head? I really *must* be tired.

Especially when I turned to see who had spoken them.

It was Steph, doing his usual appearing out of nowhere trick. He was wearing the shimmering, jewel-toned cloak of the Wizard's that aided in this magic, but even as I started to rush towards him, he had taken it off and was folding it over the back of one of the chairs. That cloak was the only touch of color he ever wore. The rest of his outfit was pure Hamlet, black boots and pants under a black tunic he wore untucked and unbelted, loose around his hips.

But the tall mass of dark curls on his head was nothing like that Danish prince. Those were all his own. And as I kissed him hello, I indulged myself in burying my hands in it. The curls always felt so cool and soft against my fingers. Even on a hot, sticky August night like the one pressing against the window behind us. And even in the perfect cool, dry interior of the bookshop.

"I thought you said you didn't mind my brother," I said to him after that quick kiss had become three longer kisses.

"Did I say that?" Steph asked.

"You did," Houdini said. "You also insisted that it was best if I didn't speak when he was here. And that you would tell me the moment you were sure it was no longer necessary."

"I know it's a hardship for you," Steph said, giving Houdini's head a quick scratch. "I promise I'm not being overly cautious. Mercutio may not currently be working as a ritual magician, but he had many close friendships with people who are. And no one is more likely to abuse a dragonet than a ritual magician gone rogue."

"So you've said," Houdini said, almost a pout. But not quite. He didn't take it lightly, everything we all did to keep him safe.

"You've still been asking about him?" I asked.

"As much as I can," Steph said. "Not that I don't trust him. But... well, I don't trust him. I mean, I *want* to."

"I know," I said, and sunk into the chair at Houdini's right hand with a sigh. "I feel the same way. But he just showed up out of nowhere, and nothing he says quite feels like the whole truth. I don't know what to make of him."

"He said he came to find you as soon as he knew you existed, right?" Steph said as he slid into the chair next to mine.

"Yeah, I guess that part felt true," I admitted. I watched as he picked up the books on the table one by one, scanning the covers without saying a word.

Then he got to the calculus book and turned to me with one eyebrow raised high.

"I know, grasping at straws," I said, folding my arms on the tabletop and burying my face into them. It would be nice to nap. My body was tired. But I knew my mind was never going to allow it.

There were still a few hours to go before dawn. I didn't see myself sleeping before then. Not even a little.

"Actually, I'm just surprised you didn't jump on that sooner," Steph said. "Higher-level math is something I've only dipped my toe into. Definitely not for me. But with the way your mind works, I think you might find it quite rewarding."

"With chaos magic?" I asked, perking up enough to lift my head.

"Well, theoretical magic, anyway," he said. "Chaos magic isn't all you can do, you know."

"Yeah," I said glumly. I fidgeted with the silver bracelet on my wrist. Before Steph and the Wizard had given it to me, I had been a constant danger to myself and others. So many things had just spontaneously caught on fire. Now the charm inside that bracelet kept the chaos inside me from growing too big for me to control.

But without it, I was just as useless with magic as I'd ever been.

"You have more general knowledge of every branch of magic still being taught in the world than any wizard I know," Steph said. He caught my hand in his and ducked his face down until our eyes met and he knew I was listening to him. "I've known a lot of wizards, Tabitha. Almost all of them currently living, actually. No one knows more than they do in their chosen fields of study. But their knowledge is by design very narrow. There are so many uses for a wider base of knowledge. I'm not sure you've thought enough about what you can do with what you know. You're still too focused on what you can't do."

I swallowed hard. Self-confidence still wasn't something I had a ton of. Not after years of acing the written tests but failing the practicals over and over again all through my academic years.

It had helped that, since coming to the Square, I had found a community where no one cared who could do how much or how little magic. We all just lived our lives knowing everyone else was doing their best. Academic life had been *nothing* like that.

And it had helped even more that I had met Audrey, my best friend and most loyal cheerleader. She did all the magic between us, but the spells she wove were the ones I designed for her. They worked like gangbusters, but she was always the first to hand all the credit to me. She just waved the wand and spoke the rhymes, she said.

Which I knew wasn't true. Not only could I not do those spells myself, I knew even if I handed them off to a different witch, the results wouldn't be as good. It wasn't Audrey's fault that her teachers in ritual magic had never found a way to explain the knowledge in a way that clicked with her.

I could. And I could write spells that really maximized her growing skills. But it was almost embarrassing, how quick she was to throw all the praise my way.

But these words from Steph were different than that. I mean, he was definitely my number two cheerleader, no question about that.

But he was also my coach. And what he was saying now was something I had literally never thought of before.

I had tried so many paths while still attending the magical academies, and every one had dead-ended on me. My last hope had been apprenticing in a library. Well, not just any library. It had been an opportunity to work at the All-Planes Athenaeum.

But my out-of-control power had put an end to that by setting fire to one of the wizards who had been evaluating my fitness for the position.

Since then, working at my uncles' bookshop had been all I had been hoping for. Hence my panic at what was going to happen tomorrow.

But Steph, in his usual gentle way, was reminding me I had other gifts. There were other paths. I hadn't tried everything yet. Not even remotely.

I put my arms around him and hugged him tight.

"Oh, thank you," Houdini said to Steph with palpable relief.

"For what?" I asked. I didn't want to stop hugging Steph, but I turned my head on his shoulder enough to look at Houdini, his snout resting on the edge of the table as he peered at both of us with his dark brown eyes.

"You've been this tense mess for days," Houdini said. "That charm on your bracelet has been throbbing like a telltale heart that's about to explode. I've been bracing for flames."

I looked down at the bracelet, resting as cooly and calmly as ever on my wrist. "That's not true," I told him.

"It's absolutely true," Houdini said with a sniff. "It's not my fault you can't sense things the way I do."

"What about you?" I asked, lifting my head to look at Steph. "What have you been sensing?"

"Nothing from your bracelet," he said. But then he touched my hair. "This has been extra interesting the last few days, though."

I put my hands on my hair and flattened it down under my palms. I hadn't noticed anything different about it at all. But I had been pretty distracted.

"Your uncles aren't going to throw you out," Steph said.

"I know that," I said, still trying to flatten my hair down. It was a little extra full, as if I'd spent the whole day outside in the heat rather than in the cool interior of the bookshop.

"And even if they did, there's plenty of room in the Tower," Steph went on. "Not only would you be welcome, I'm afraid the Wizard would insist on you staying close. With us, if need be. Although I'm sure Audrey would fight us for the right to take you in."

"I know I'm nervous, and I know it's irrational, okay?" I said, forcing my hands to drop back into my lap. But then I reached up again to adjust the frame of my glasses just a little. That gesture was one my uncle had taught me. He insisted it was calming. I still did it, even though I didn't find it as effective as he apparently did.

"Is your brother being here helping or hurting?" Steph asked, his tone carefully neutral.

"He's trying to help," I said. "The fact that he wants to try kind of does help. Honestly, I'm feeling better now than I was an hour ago."

"Ask her if she intends to sleep at all tonight," Houdini said. I glanced over to see his head had disappeared from view. He was curled up on the padded seat of his chair, apparently accepting that our bed was not where we were heading any time soon.

"I'm not going to ask that," Steph said to me with a conspiratorial smile. "But I do have something else to ask. I meant to be here sooner, but I got caught up with an experiment with the Wizard. I missed dinner entirely. Are you up for ordering a pizza?"

"Absolutely," I said. "But I'm warning you now, I'm going to want pineapple on it."

"Well, I was going to insist if you didn't," Steph said. "Nothing better than a little citrus to take the edge off all the grease, right?"

"Right," I said, even as I pulled out my phone.

Houdini made a sound in the back of my mind like a long-tortured sigh. But he wasn't fooling anyone. When the pizza came, he'd be begging for bits of sausage as vociferously as any real dog.

But I was already ordering extra sausage on the app. *Extra* extra, so I could scrape some off onto a plate of his own.

A dragon needed a little dignity, after all.

THREE

Steph hung around until nearly dawn, but couldn't go with me to wait at the portal for my uncles to return. His master, the Wizard, needed him at the Tower, which probably meant another trip across the globe.

Having zipped to Europe and back with him a couple of times the month before, I didn't know how he could stand doing it so often. It was exhausting, worse than jet lag, and I had not even been the one exerting any magical power to do it. I had just been along for the ride.

So it was just Houdini and me walking through the hedge maze in the gray early morning. The heat wasn't too bad that early in the day, but the humidity from the day before lingered still, coating the grass underfoot and the leaves of the hedges all around us in a kind of moisture that lacked all the charms of dew or even frost. It was just... gross.

When we reached the portal that stood in the open space at the heart of the maze, I realized we weren't the only ones waiting for the scheduled arrival of the magic streams that conveyed witches around the world. There were two young people sitting on crates of mail, yawning hugely and not quite chatting with each other. I recognized the boy from the last time I had traveled through this portal and he had been doing the same job, but the girl beside him only gave me the vague sense of someone I had seen around the Square now and again. They both gave me and Houdini a tired nod, then went back to their whispered conversation.

"Do you think your uncle will remember me?" Houdini asked me. He sounded terribly anxious. I looked down at him sitting on the wet grass beside me. His big brown eyes were gazing up at me, his ears flat back against his skull in that way that always made me want to pick him up and cuddle his worries away.

But I resisted the temptation. "Carlo? I didn't know you'd ever even met," I said. "I mean, he knows I am your legal guardian now that Agatha has passed. He's not going to be surprised to see you."

"We met a few times," Houdini said. But I could hear hedging in his voice. Even though it was only in my mind, that voice.

"And?" I prompted, not quite smiling. I had a feeling I already knew where this was going.

"I might have been... unmannerly," he said, dropping his eyes and hanging his head just a little.

"Like Titus Bloom levels of unmannerly?" I asked. Titus Bloom owned the Bitter Brew Coffeeshop, the Square's chief competitor to the Loose Leaves Teashop, once Agatha's but now her grandniece Audrey's. When I had first met Houdini, back when I thought he was just the dog he appeared to be, he had nursed a particular grudge against Titus Bloom. He would growl at the mere sight of him passing by the teashop doors, a growl that would erupt into a barrage of barking that always felt like a lot, coming from that little body.

Not that he'd been entirely wrong to be suspicious. Titus Bloom had indeed been trying to acquire the teashop real estate from Agatha. But the real thing that had set Houdini off had been a strange smell he couldn't place but instinctively distrusted. It turned out in the end what he was smelling was actually emanating from

Titus' wife Nell, who had been making ill-advised bargains with a certain otherworldly entity.

That entity had killed Agatha, at Nell's behest. But Titus had been blameless in all of it.

Well, if you considered someone who really ought to have been at least a smidge suspicious of what his wife was up to blameless.

I had stopped blaming him myself. But I wouldn't exactly call us friends.

But Houdini made a snorting noise, both a little doggy one and a more disdainful one in the voice that spoke inside my mind. "Not remotely. But still. Do you think he remembers?"

"If he does, we can explain you were a littler guy then. You've learned a lot since then. I see no reason why he wouldn't agree to a fresh start," I said. But after a moment's thought, I felt compelled to add, "Unless there was biting involved?"

"No, never!" Houdini said with a snort of offense. "Only I worry that he won't let you stay because it means I have to stay too."

Those ears were plastered back against his skull again, his mournful eyes bigger than ever, and I gave up trying to preserve his dignity. He allowed me to scoop him up and cuddle him close, even burying his little head under my chin to press his nose close to my neck.

"We're going to be just fine," I promised him.

"I wouldn't mind so much, living in the Tower," he murmured. "If we have to. But I know you'd very much prefer the bookshop."

I didn't answer, just stroked his back until his chihuahua trembling settled back down.

Then the pinkening sky just visible between the curved arched pillars of stone that defined the area of the portal began to glow with magical energy. That glow brightened, then began to swirl like a vortex. The two young people waiting on the crates hopped down to the ground and picked up the first of the packages, ready to toss them inside the portal the moment it was properly open.

The heart of that glowing vortex elongated like a cat's eye, then opened up with a rush of colors like the world's most intense rainbow. Then two shapes emerged, both men of average height but heavy set, their rounded bellies not quite covered by their faded sweater vests.

Sweater vests, despite the heat of August, which I was sure was no less intense in the city in the south of France they were leaving behind than it was here in Minneapolis. But it brought a smile to my face all the same. My uncles. They absolutely hadn't changed.

"Ah, Tabitha!" my uncle Carlo said, adjusting the frames of his square steel glasses as if to be sure it really was me standing there waiting for him. Frank, behind him, gave me a tired nod of hello, but then turned back to the portal to catch the first of what turned out to be nearly a dozen suitcases.

They had left home with only two over-stuffed bags apiece.

"Successful trips acquiring things for the bookshop?" I asked as I set Houdini down so I could help move the suitcases out of the way so the two young people on mail duty wouldn't trip over them as they tossed package after package into that rainbow-filled cat's eye.

"Very successful," Carlo said with a weary smile. "It's going to take us most of the rest of the week just to catalog it all, I fear. But we're eager to get to it. We've found some really interesting things, books and artifacts both."

"That's good," I said as cheerily as I could. But my heart was sinking.

They were planning to get back to work right away. I had been holding onto a hope I hadn't even expressed to myself that they'd want a few extra days to recover from the trip, but that hope was dashed now.

But my self-preoccupied thoughts were interrupted by Frank pulling me into a tight hug. He always gave the best hugs, like sinking into the embrace of a larger-than-life teddy bear.

"Thank you for making this possible, Tabitha," he said when he finally released me. There was real emotion there in his brown eyes, like he was about to be overcome with tears.

"Yes, thank you, Tabitha," Carlo said. Then he seemed to notice Houdini there for the first time. He looked down at the little dog, adjusting his glasses to sit more squarely on his nose. "And you, Houdini. I'm sure you were a help to Tabitha while we were away. Weren't you?"

Houdini looked up at me as if asking for permission.

"It's up to you," was all I said out loud to the dog. But what I really wanted to say was something more like, "It's my uncle. It's not Mercutio."

Houdini looked up at Carlo, his ears in full radar dish deployment. Then he spoke in his most formal cadence, in my mind, but also in the minds of both of my uncles. I could tell by the way their faces lit up that they could hear him.

"I am very sorry for my behavior when I was younger. I was a foolish dragonet, perhaps too afraid of things that were no threat to me or to Agatha. I hope we can start again now that I am older and wiser."

Carlo blinked at him wordlessly. Frank swallowed hard, then whispered, "Did he just say drag—"

But Carlo cut him off before he could get the whole word out, "It's going to take a few trips to get this all into the bookshop, let alone all the way upstairs. Let's get started, shall we?"

Then he gave Frank an intense look which Frank seemed to understand at once. Frank gave Houdini a single nervous glance, but then just nodded to Carlo and bent to lift the largest of the suitcases first.

I grabbed the largest one I thought I could reasonably manage, regretting once more that Steph hadn't been able to stay. His teleportation magic would've really come in handy in that moment.

"I was hoping Mercutio would be here," Carlo said to me as we fell into step shoulder to shoulder, following Frank through the maze, back to the bookshop.

"I think he still feels weird about things," I said. "You really had no idea he even existed?"

"I really didn't," he said with a sigh. "Your mother, my sister, she kept a lot of secrets. But I never thought she'd keep one so huge. But he certainly must know he's welcome here."

"I've told him so," I assured him. "I guess he'll come around when he's ready."

I didn't mention my feeling, like Mercutio was avoiding the interior of the Square for some reason. I had nothing to back it up, after all. It was just my gut whispering to me.

Then Carlo said, "I hope you don't mind that Frank and I wanted to get back into the shop right away today. We just want to power through the exhaustion as much as we can and get on a normal sleep schedule as soon as possible. I mean, in all likelihood, we'll be crashing halfway through dinner tonight, if not sooner."

He ended with a laugh that I tried to join in on. But it sounded false in my ears.

But he didn't seem to hear it, just went on with what he was saying, "We'll have to draw up a schedule at some point before the weekend, of course. We don't want to monopolize all of your time. I know you've been keeping yourself busy helping out all around the Square. But Frank and I really appreciate having you here. It's going to give us so much more time to really focus on our own projects without dealing with customer interruptions. It's worth more than gold, I tell you, distraction-free time."

I swallowed hard. I could scarcely believe what I was hearing. But it made total sense. Having worked in the bookshop all by myself for three months, I could see how it was a lot even for two people to handle seven days a week, fifty-two weeks a year.

"Of course," was all I could trust my voice to squeak out. But Carlo just gave me a fond smile.

Then he looked down at Houdini trotting close to my heels. "All is, of course, forgiven, my little dragonet. You are welcome in our home for as long as you wish to stay."

"Thank you," Houdini said with a little bow of his head.

Then Carlo turned his attention back to me.

"I know we have a lot to discuss, the two of us, about your mother and the rest of our family. I promised I would tell you all I knew when I was home, and that time has come," he said. But I could hear the reluctance he was trying not to show. He had agreed, but he hadn't exactly liked it.

Plus, I was pretty sure from conversations we'd had over the phone over the summer that he was under a powerful spell. There were a lot of things he wouldn't even be able to tell me. That spell wouldn't let him. And if he pushed to try anyway, I still wasn't sure just what might happen.

But I knew I didn't really want to find out. It could be bad.

"Perhaps we can wait to get into it until after you've met Mercutio," I said. "It involves him too, after all. And I know he'll want to be a part of that conversation."

"Of course," Carlo said.

I could tell how badly he wanted to adjust his glasses again, a nervous gesture that always calmed him. But the suitcase in his arms had grown heavier even as mine had, and he couldn't spare a hand to do it.

Luckily, we were nearly out of the hedge maze. I could see the rising brick wall of the bookshop over the less immaculately groomed tops of the hedges before us.

Only three more trips to fetch the rest of the luggage. Then I had something I hadn't had in months: a guilt-free day to spend all the hours I wanted with my friends.

And that would start as my days always did, with tea and scones in the teashop.

Today, I couldn't wait.

CHAPTER

FOUR

Nothing in the world smelled better than Audrey's teashop in the morning. When we gathered for breakfast, it was always an hour before she opened for business, but after she'd finished her baking for the day. Her display case was filled with scones, cookies and bars for humans as well as baked treats just for dogs, which always smelled just as tempting as the human snacks.

And our little circle of friends got to sample it all when it was fresh from the oven.

While I lingered just inside the door on the Square side of the shop, breathing in all the smells—letting the baked good aromas settle until I could discern the subtler scents of tea leaves and spices, trying to guess what blend was brewing in the pot already wrapped in a tea towel and waiting on our customary table—Houdini skittered past me, racing for the water bowl that Audrey always left full of fresh, clean water. She really put every effort in to luring the many locals who passed by her door while out walking their dogs.

But it wasn't water that Houdini was eager to sample. He just knew that from that position, Audrey could see him from wherever she was standing behind the counter. And indeed she did, setting a platter of scones down on the counter and taking two of the dog treats out of the display case. Her long blonde hair swung in straight wings to either side of her face as she bent to offer the first of the treats to Houdini.

Who was really working the dog act, dancing on his hind legs and pawing at Audrey's knee. But she didn't let him have the treat until he jumped for it. Then she laughed as he jumped again, snagging the second treat out of her other hand.

"He's got a five foot vertical leap, I swear," she said as she picked up the platter again and brought it to the table. Then she leaned close to my ear to whisper, "Liam brought your brother with him. They're in the back, putting my dairy delivery into the fridge for me."

"Great," I said. Because it was good news. I had been half afraid that with my uncles back, Mercutio would just disappear. But he hadn't.

Of course, the real reason Audrey had whispered that to me was to remind me, as well as sharp-eared Houdini, that he was confined to dog behavior for the morning. No sitting at the table and eating off his own plate, and absolutely no talking to us.

Not that he had a particularly good track record with remaining silent. I mean, he tried. But he always had opinions. Audrey and I were pretty good at not reacting when he spoke to us, but it was still a new experience for Liam, who hadn't even known that we were witches or that magic was real until just a few months before. He tried to school his features into a poker face too, but I had seen Mercutio shoot him curious glances on more than one occasion.

I didn't think my brother was truly suspicious yet. But I knew if he did get suspicious, he was all too well equipped to find answers. Better that Houdini remained firmly a dog in his mind.

"What's on the menu this morning?" I asked as I slid into my usual spot.

"Nothing too fancy," Audrey said. "The sweet scones are chocolate cherry, and the savory are zucchini and fresh herbs. Houdini just had a bacon and pumpkin treat, which he seems to be enjoying immensely. And the tea is just an Irish breakfast blend, because I had a craving."

"I kind of want one of Houdini's treats," Liam said as he emerged from the back room, my brother close behind him.

You couldn't find two more opposite-looking young men than my brother and Audrey's boyfriend, Liam. My brother was tall and pale with all of that long dark hair swinging loose in luscious waves that put even Audrey's blonde locks to shame. But now that I had noticed it, he really was almost too buff to pass for a vampire.

A vampire hunter, maybe. The kind that was secretly half-vampire.

Liam, on the other hand, was of average height but looked short next to Mercutio. His blonde hair was a shade darker than Audrey's, but his usual soft, wavy curls were not responding to the humidity outside well at all. He was bordering on my own chaotic hair look. And he definitely had the body type of a guy more comfortable with books and computers than sporting equipment of any variety.

Of course, the more striking differences between the two weren't the visible ones. Liam was from the prosaic world, and a small town out on the prairie of western Minnesota at that. Mercutio wasn't just a witch, he was one who had trained in the most elite forms of magic. And he had grown up in the most cosmopolitan of homes, always in the hearts of the world's biggest cities, attending the elitist of academies, carrying on our father's last name of Ward, the name of the prominent family I had never been acknowledged by.

And yet, in the last month, Mercutio and Liam had become fast friends. They were roommates, living a short walk away in a loft apartment in a renovated building that had once been a flour mill. It was a tight space for two people to share, but they didn't seem to mind it at all.

Which made sense with Liam. His last place had been a two-bedroom apartment he'd shared with five other guys, and then five other guys plus one guy's girlfriend. The loft was downright spacious after that, with so much more privacy than he'd had before.

But Mercutio? For the life of me, I couldn't see why he was so content with where he was. He had last lived in a penthouse in Chicago, one of the magically hidden spaces that lurked in the corners of the prosaic world through a complex web of spells that required resource-intensive magical maintenance almost constantly. Not cheap. I had never seen it, but I had seen similar apartments in the hidden floors atop the Foshay Tower in Minneapolis. I could well imagine what he'd left behind. And what still waited for him, whenever he chose to return.

And I'd seen the loft. In the corner of the loft's only room, they had bunk beds. To call their bathroom rudimentary would be to do it a kindness it absolutely did not deserve. It was separated from the rest of the space by a mere curtain. The dingiest shower curtain I had ever seen. And their only window looked out on the brick wall of the next building over, a mere foot and a half away. Sunlight just barely filtered in.

And yet I didn't think he was lying when he said he was completely content. I just wished it made some kind of sense.

I came out of my personal reverie as Audrey poured tea into my teacup, but when I murmured my thanks to her, I realized she was distracted as well. Although whatever was on her mind seemed more upsetting than my own puzzling thoughts had been.

"What is it?" I asked.

She started to shake her head as if to tell me it was nothing. But then she changed her mind, setting the teapot down on its ceramic coaster, then sitting close beside me. "It's Barnardo. He's not here."

"He's not that late," I said, glancing at the clock. It was only a few minutes after seven. The teashop didn't open until eight. He had tons of time.

And the longer he took to arrive, the better, really. Because he always brought his black Siamese Miss Snooty Cat with him. And Miss Snooty Cat went out of her way to be rude to Houdini.

Not that she was a cat anymore than Houdini was a dog. No, she was a malevolent sort of creature called a matagot who had struck up some sort of magically binding deal with Barnardo's now-deceased father. She had remained with Barnardo after his father had passed, but I had no idea what the real arrangement was between them. I wasn't even sure if Barnardo realized she wasn't really a cat.

He was so protective of her, I was loath to bring it up. But I was admittedly a bit relieved every time Houdini and I came down to the teashop and he wasn't there.

But I was just remembering as Audrey said, "He wasn't here yesterday. Or the day before, either."

"Yeah, you're right," I said with a frown. "That is weird. Have you heard from him at all?"

"Not a word," she said. Then she gave me an anxious look. "Should we be worried?"

"No, not yet," I said. "It's too soon for that. But I have the day off, so if you like after we finish eating, I can go upstairs and check in with him. Just to make sure he's okay."

"Would you?" she said with immense relief. "I'd appreciate that so much." She started to turn her attention to the scones on her plate when she suddenly spun back to me to say, "Wait! Your uncles are back this morning, aren't they? I can't believe I forgot! I'm such a bad friend."

"Don't be silly. You were worried about Barnardo, on top of running a business single-handedly," I said. "I think I can live with you remembering a mere five minutes after I came into your shop."

"How are they? How was their trip?" she asked. Then she shot a look over at Mercutio and Liam—deep in some conversation I couldn't even imagine the topic of—before leaning closer to me to ask, "They are letting you stay, right?"

"Yes, I am staying," I said with a wide grin I couldn't possibly suppress even if I had wanted to. "We're going to have a rotating schedule for working the register and handling the customers. That will leave them time to work on their own little research projects—I don't even know the details on those, but I'm dying to ask. And that will leave me with time to work on my magic control with the Wizard."

"And to solve mysteries," Liam put in. Apparently, he and Mercutio had ended their conversation in time to catch at least part of what I was saying to Audrey. But me seeing the Wizard wasn't really a secret.

"Hopefully those won't keep coming up," I said. But I could see that worried frown creasing Audrey's brow again.

Liam noticed it, too. When he didn't ask what was bothering her, I realized the two of them must have already discussed it. A quiet fell over the table, as none of us knew what to say next. Then Liam broke it by saying, "Tabitha. I have a book for you."

"A book?" I said, a touch too eagerly. I wish I could say I was relieved for the change of topic, but honestly I just always over-react to the idea that someone is about to hand me a book I've not met before.

"Does she need another book?" Mercutio asked with a dry grin.

"She might need this one," Liam said to him as he dug through the bag he had left on a chair nearby. He came out with a battered leather-bound book with thick, coarse pages that had been bound by the printer and then inexpertly cut by the first recipient, leaving very jagged edges.

But I could tell even before I touched it that those cuts had been made centuries before. I inhaled the pulpy smell of the paper, the dry smell of leather that would be just perfect synthesized into a cologne, and the faint hint of old glue.

"Where did you get this?" I asked, still holding the book flat on my palms as I took in deep breaths of its particular scent.

"Aren't you going to open it?" Mercutio asked, still amused.

But Liam ignored him. "You know I'm working overnight security at the university, right?"

I did indeed know that. I had tweaked a spell designed to help a witch choose a path so that it would function for a job-hunting prosaic like Liam. Audrey had performed it with him, and the very next day he'd finally gotten a call-back from an interview.

He was much more excited at working overnight security at the university than I would've expected. But on top of that, he could afford half the rent on that loft apartment. He'd only been working that job for a few weeks, but he was in much better spirits than I'd seen him all summer.

But he was still explaining about the book in my hands. "Part of my patrol is through the acquisitions library. Shelves upon shelves of books that they've received as donations from dead people's estates that haven't been processed yet. No one even knows that book exists. But I thought you might like to see it."

"Hold on. You stole from the place you're meant to be guarding?" Mercutio asked.

Liam's cheeks flushed crimson. "I borrowed," he said stiffly.

But I knew even before opening the cover that whatever I was holding, it was very important indeed. Liam might be fast and loose with some rules, but only for very good causes. Like solving murders.

Or, in this case, like finding out someone's lost identity.

Because what I was holding was a book on dragons. Only this was no ordinary prosaic book about dragons. I knew at once that the text I was scanning was real information, things only magical people knew about dragons, and very few of those knew this much.

There were a thousand pages to be read and examined. And those pages were very dense. It was a lot.

I didn't want to be too hopeful that there would be real answers here. But it was hard not to be. The book I was holding practically radiated its veracity, its importance, its power.

"Where did you get this?" I asked him, barely breathing out the words.

"I just grabbed it about an hour ago, but if you want, I can trace what estate it came from when I get to work tonight," he said. "Tabitha, it really is just a loan. I have to put it back before anyone misses it. But it felt like a crime, leaving it there where no one would ever appreciate what it truly was. Not the way you can."

"I'll make a copy," I told him even as I pressed that tome to my chest and wrapped my arms around it tightly. "As quickly as I can. Thank you so much for this, Liam. Honestly. This is going to help. I just know it."

"Help with what?" Mercutio pressed.

"It's for a friend," I told him. "It's a confidence I can't break, as Liam well knows, so don't try twisting his arm to get it out of him, either."

"I would never," Mercutio said. In that moment, he reminded me exactly of Houdini. Houdini could utter those exactly same words with the same air of personal offense.

And I knew in both cases, they were only offended because I had caught them out before they could do what we both knew full well they were planning to do.

Not that it mattered. Short of deploying magic, nothing Mercutio did would get Liam to betray me or Houdini.

And given the magical oath Liam had sworn to Steph, maybe not even if he tried magic. Our secret was safe with Liam.

But that look of suspicion I had been so eager to keep out of Mercutio's eyes was there now. And I couldn't move that clock back.

I just had to hope this book was worth it.

CHAPTER

FIVE

I had spent many a long day sitting at the study table in my nook on the fourth floor of the Weal & Woe Bookshop, but this day was different from any of the others.

Because, for once, I didn't have to respond every time I heard the bell over the prosaic door ring or sensed the presence of a more magical person appearing somewhere in the stacks. I could just focus on the book in front of me and nothing else.

Which might have been more possible if it had been an ordinary day. But apparently word had gotten out that my uncles were back and in the bookshop. The bell rang constantly as prosaic customer after prosaic customer came in. I'm sure they all bought books, because the regular customers were the kind of people who could never leave a bookshop without acquiring a new stack of To Be Reads. But they were really coming in to chat with my uncles.

And even with my limited magical skills, I could sense the presence of other witches and wizards lurking among the stacks. Only the most sensitive of prosaic shoppers were even aware that there was more than one level to the bookshop, and those that noticed the central staircase were always told the upper level was for storage only.

But in fact, only the seventh level at the very top was full of boxed books waiting to be shelved. The five levels in between were packed with books, scrolls, manuscripts, and a variety of rare artifacts, all available for purchase. The bookshop's magical customers were seldom browsers, though. They came in for something specific, and they knew how to sense when the bookshop was guiding them about. I had quickly learned the art of being near if I was needed, but not interrupting when someone was on a shopping quest.

That day, the shelves were packed with magical shoppers who really did feel like they were just browsing, killing time while they waited for the prosaic crowd to break up around the front desk so they could chat a little more freely with my uncles.

It was a lot to tune out.

But the book I had laying open before me was engrossing enough for me to barely need the bookshop to do its little magic, steering shoppers away from my nook and towards their own goals and muffling the sounds of their voices and footfalls to a soft murmur.

"This is better than the other books?" Houdini asked. He was sitting on the chair next to mine, but he was draped over the arm of that chair to rest his chin on the back of my wrist. I doubted that was particularly comfortable, but he didn't seem to mind. It was apparently preferable to his first position, sitting on the center of the table and looking down at the pages upside-down. "How is that possible? Isn't it a prosaic book?"

"No," I said, but I drawled that single word out. I wasn't entirely sure that was true. "It's not magical in and of itself, anyway."

"Oh, surely not," Houdini quickly agreed. "I would've sensed at once if it had been anything like the books Agatha wrote and left for Audrey."

"Right," I agreed. Those books had been filled with hidden pages or extra recipes written in invisible ink underneath the more mundane recipes. And that was leaving aside the truly important tome, which had been written in a spell-code that had taken Audrey and me both working together to break.

This was just text on a page, with illustrations. There was no copyright information in it, but I guessed from the materials in its construction and the qualities of its typeset and illustrations that it dated to the early 1800s. I wanted to say it was also from Scotland, but without double-checking a few things, I couldn't be totally confident in that assessment.

But I was pretty sure I was right, even though the author's name didn't narrow it down much. I mean, John Carter, once I wrestled my brain away from constantly adding "of Mars" to it, is a pretty generic name. The man could've been Scottish, or Irish, or English.

"But how is this going to help?" Houdini asked. I had leaned in over the page to examine one of the illustrations more closely, but sat back to look down into his dark brown eyes. He was worried, that was clear.

"The other books we've gone through have made us both experts on all the varieties of dragons in history, and how to tell them apart, right?" I said.

"For all the help that is," he grumbled, and shook his paw as if something stuck to it was annoying him. Or perhaps it was the paw itself he was trying to shake away.

But I took his point.

"Yes, but this John Carter fellow was specifically working to create a taxonomy of dragon *artifacts*," I said, tapping the illustration I had been studying. "Granted, there aren't many of them around here on Earth. But he tracked down all he could. And his research on each of them is very, very thorough. These chapters are organized by his research trips. Look, these are things he found in Transylvania. But I really wished he had written down dates. It's almost like he deliberately didn't, for some reason."

"Is there anything in there about other planes of existence?" Houdini asked.

Which was a good question. We knew for a fact that his dragon family had been traveling along magical paths and had been pulled off course by the power of the Tower. What we didn't know was how Houdini had gotten separated from the others, or if he was the only one who even touched down on Earth. It seemed likely he had been. Nothing else had been there when Agatha had sensed his presence and retrieved him, still wet and surrounded by the fractured remains of his shell.

"Maybe," I said, flipping through the pages towards the back of the book. "Or he might mention the other planes when he's describing the individual artifacts. There's no way to really scan this book like that. I'm just going to have to sit down and read the whole thing."

"Before Liam has to put it back?" Houdini asked.

"No, I know Steph will have a way to make a copy or two. I'm sure the Wizard will want one for his own library. But they're out for the day, so I'll have to ask him when they're back," I said.

"I'm sure he'll be willing and able to help," Houdini said with that total confidence he always showed in Steph. Not that it was misplaced or anything. Or that it didn't make sense he didn't have the same confidence in me.

But it still hurt a little bit. I had been working so hard to control my magic on my own, without needing the restraint of the charmed bracelet on my wrist. But there was always so much more to learn.

"Right," I said, forcing my mind back on the book itself. "So anyway, this John Carter was trying to assign dragon artifacts to the types of dragon he thought had left them behind. He has a ton of notes, and it looks like there are even some charts in the back."

"Different types of dragons vary a bit in size and color," Houdini said as much to himself as to me. "They vary more in average intelligence and, relatedly, level of magical skill. But the most distinctive characteristic that varies between types is the magical breath."

"Right," I said. "But you don't have access to that in your current form, and we can't rely on your color or size to tell us anything about what you might have looked like before Agatha disguised you."

I looked down at him, waiting for him to come to the same conclusion I already had.

He blinked slowly, then looked away from me and towards the open pages of the book. The illustration on the right-hand page was of a dragon with a long, snake-like body and forked appendages running down its back in a bristling row. All the illustrations were in black and white, of course, but the caption on this one pointed out that it was indeed a drawing of a black dragon.

"You think measuring my intelligence and magical skill will help?" he finally asked.

"Maybe not measure, not quantitatively," I hedged. My school-days might be firmly in my past now, but the memory of starting at a new academy with a battery of tests meant to quantify what I knew was still too raw. I would never do that to Houdini. "No, I was thinking more of a qualitative assessment."

"I don't follow you," Houdini said.

"Look, here," I said, pointing to the text on the left-hand side of the page. "This particular set of artifacts he found in Transylvania included a large array of scrolls dedicated to the Greeks' under-standing of mathematics and astronomy. John Carter concluded they likely belonged to the hoard of a black dragon because they are known to have a great interest in such matters."

"I don't know if this is going to help," Houdini said after a moment's thought. "My interests have been shaped very much by what Agatha was interested in, and then what you and Audrey are interested in. I'm not sure if I even know *what* I'm interested in."

"That might be a bad example," I said with a sigh. "And anyway, I'm not sure I'm the one to figure this all out for you. I was hoping to ask the Wizard."

"Oh, that's a fine idea," Houdini agreed. "He does a great many experiments. He will know just how to structure a test that will yield the best possible results."

"I thought the same," I said.

"But they aren't back yet?" he asked.

"No, not yet," I said with a laugh.

"That's a pity," he said. Then, this time with just a hint of smugness to his tone, he said, "I can't wait to find out what I really am. And do you know what I'm going to do first when I do find out?"

"Try to contact your family?"

"Certainly," Houdini said, too quickly. Clearly, that hadn't been what he was thinking of at all.

"And second?" I asked. I couldn't help the fond smile that crept over my face. But the smug demeanor radiating from the tiny body was really just too adorable.

"I'm going to tell Miss Snooty Cat that I never needed her help at all," he said. Then he actually sniffed and put his nose up in the air. A remarkably good imitation of the cat in question.

But my smile melted away. I couldn't share his moment of smug humor, as well-earned as I knew it was. Miss Snooty Cat had indeed been just awful to him when she refused to tell him what she had learned about him.

Because the mention of her name reminded me of what I had forgotten: that we hadn't seen Barnardo in two days.

And Audrey was worried about him.

And I had promised to check in with him right after breakfast.

I glanced at the time on my cellphone and sucked in a frustrated breath. Lunchtime had come and gone while I had been poring over that book.

"Houdini, I've got to go," I said.

"If you're going near her, I'd prefer to stay here," he said, hopping into the seat of my chair the minute I vacated it so he could sit in front of the open book on his own. "I'd rather not see her again until I can lord it over her."

"Of course," I said. "If Steph comes, can you ask him about copying the book?"

"I can and shall," Houdini said, then put his paws on the table so he could lean close over the same illustration of a black dragon I had been perusing.

I certainly hoped Houdini wasn't one of those. There was something treacherous in the demeanor of that dragon, slinking through upthrust rocks with narrowed eyes that screamed untrustworthiness to me.

But I said nothing, just kissed Houdini on the top of his head, then ran down the stairs to the main level.

It made no sense to hurry now. If anything had happened to Barnardo, it had happened long before breakfast, let alone in the hours since then.

And yet, something was whispering in my mind, over and over again, that I had to hurry.

I had to hurry, or it would be too late.

CHAPTER

SIX

That feeling of urgency morphed into a dread the minute I stepped out into the Square. And I was pretty sure that had nothing to do with the oppressive wave of heat and humidity that greeted me as soon as I stepped outside.

I hovered uncertainly on the bookshop's back step. I was almost tempted to run back inside. Maybe it made sense to wait until Steph was back.

I really wanted to wait until Steph was back.

But I had no idea when that was going to happen. And that dread was just a veneer over the deeper surface feelings that I really had to hurry.

So I started moving again, but not towards the stairs to the second level of the Square where the apartments began.

No, I headed to the teashop.

It was midafternoon, but no one was inside the cool teashop interior when I burst in through the doors. The tables were bare save for the tiny floral arrangements on each, their surfaces wiped clean long enough ago that no trace of liquid remained.

And while the scent of scones and a variety of teas was still thick on the air, there was nothing fresh, nothing currently putting more of itself out there.

I crossed the room to the counter where Audrey already stood, watching me approach. She was tucking her hair behind her ears, always a sign that she was nervous.

"You feel it too?" She said to me at once.

"I don't know what I feel," I said. But that wasn't exactly true. "Well, it's both urgency and dread, which is weird. But it feels like it's coming from outside of me? And I don't understand that at all."

"Me too," Audrey said with a little smile of relief that neither of us were going crazy. But that smile quickly melted away. "We should go up and see, don't you think?"

"Yeah," I agreed.

She brushed past me to the door on the prosaic world side of the teashop and locked it, then turned the sign to *closed*. Then she nodded her head towards the other door and the two of us went back out into the thick midafternoon August heat.

"It hit me all of a sudden," she said.

"Me too, the minute I stepped outside," I said.

"I had just finished washing the lunch rush dishes and was wondering what to do next," she said. "Then... bam."

"I've never really seen Barnardo do any magic," I said. "I mean, he has magic things. Especially his food service stuff. That's all clearly enchanted. But this thing in my head or heart or whatever? I don't know. Does it feel like Barnardo to you?"

"Not really," she said. We had reached the bottom of the cast-iron staircase and jogged up to the second floor before she went on. "Maybe it's Miss Snooty Cat? I know you said she was a matagot or whatever, but I've never felt anything like this from her either."

"It's strange," I said.

Barnardo's apartment was on the southeast corner of the Square, directly over the teashop. He had windows that overlooked the same street as the window in my nook in the bookshop, but also that overlooked the prosaic alley that led past the comic book store to the magically hidden base of the Tower.

And I still had no idea how he had paid for it. It was a prime piece of real estate in the magical world. As much as it had been his father's before he had died, and Barnardo had moved in to take care of his father in his last days, since he had been living in downtown Minneapolis before coming back to the Square, it was still a valid question. Those places were even harder to afford than this one.

Audrey and I had come to a halt before the door, but neither of us made a move to knock. We just stood there, sweating uselessly in the sweltering heat.

The cast-iron balcony that stood outside of Barnardo's front door was overgrown with long tendrils of some sort of ivy that seemed to love the weather. Its waxy green leaves were spread wide to soak up the sun and the moist heat. But the smell of the whitish flowers that hid behind those leaves was too cloying for my taste. Especially in that still air.

"We have to," Audrey whispered.

I nodded. But still, neither of us moved.

Then I felt something like a squeeze around my wrist. The silver bracelet there was making its presence felt, a cool touch of metal that accompanied something much less like a voice in my head than when Houdini spoke to me. But its question was, as always, perfectly clear to me.

Did I want it to release its hold on me? To let me access all of my powers of chaos?

Despite the heat, I shivered at that thought in my mind. Nothing good ever came of unleashing my power. I mean, it had saved my life, more than once. But the means to that end had been... messy.

I bit my lip hard enough to taste coppery blood, then leaned forward to knock loudly on the door.

That knock seemed to break the spell both Audrey and I had been caught in. The smell of the flowers faded away, and a breeze washed over us, almost too cool as it carried our sweat away. And it cleared all of those strange feelings out of my mind. I felt myself again.

But one thing the knock didn't do was bring anyone inside the apartment to the door.

I knocked again, more easily this time, then dug a tissue out of my pocket to dab at my bleeding lip. Audrey caught herself chewing at her own lip as she watched me and quickly shifted to tucking her hair back behind her ears again.

I knocked a third time. But there was still no answer.

"Now is the time I realize I have no idea who the landlord is in this place," I said with a humorless laugh.

"It's a sort of commune," Audrey said. "With a committee. I'm on it, actually. But I don't have a key to Barnardo's place. I'm not sure if anyone does. Maybe Titus."

I had no desire to go see Titus. Especially not on the strength of a "maybe."

But Audrey was already pulling out her wand. I stepped back as she sang a little incantation. It wasn't a spell I had ever learned, but I recognized the language as an early variant of Norse.

Then she gave the doorknob the softest of taps before tucking her wand away again.

"You know, I'm not sure if this is what Odin and Njord would consider a matter of 'safe passage'," I mused.

But when she reached for the doorknob, it turned easily at her touch.

"I went a little off book," she said with a shrug. Then she pointed a mock-accusatory finger at me. "You've been rubbing off on me, you know."

"No, you're right," I said. "I'm kind of jealous. I mean, I wished I had thought of it."

"We used something like it in school, to get past the security patrol when we wanted to sneak into the kitchen for a midnight snack," she said.

But then all the merriment went out of both of us. It was probably the word "snack" that had done it. But whatever the reason, we both remembered why we were there.

She nodded for me to go in first, and I slipped into the cool, dark interior of Barnardo's apartment.

"Barnardo?" I called as Audrey slipped in beside me, then closed the door behind us. Softly, as if she were afraid we were disturbing Barnardo's nap time.

Although I had just been wondering why all the curtains were pulled closed. Maybe he was sick?

"Barnardo?" I called again, a bit louder this time. The living room was remarkable only for the scant amount of dust that covered the coffee table. The end tables had a coating as well, although being a lighter wood, they didn't show it so much.

Still, Barnardo was a diligent housekeeper. Any dust at all was unusual.

But more unusual: there wasn't any hint of cat hair. And by the time this much dust settled, cat hair should've long ago become a more serious problem.

Audrey inclined her head towards the kitchen, and I nodded. Then we walked together through the cramped corner that was laid out as a dining room, although in all my months in the Square I had never seen Barnardo use it as such.

Then we were in the open doorway that led into the kitchen, and there was no longer any need to go further into the apartment.

We'd found Barnardo and Miss Snooty Cat both. They were sprawled out on the linoleum floor. Between Miss Snooty Cat's food and water dishes was a small saucer with a congealed puddle of cream in it. And next to Barnardo's outstretched hand was an over-turned glass bottle of the same. Cream had spilled out of it, forming a large lake that had spread out until it was soaking his sleeve and the hair of Miss Snooty Cat's belly both.

I don't know why that sight struck me the way it did. I had seen blood pool like that before. But somehow this sight of cream all over

Barnardo's kitchen was so much worse than blood. So much more... not right.

We were both transfixed in that doorway for far too long. Like if we made any kind of move, then everything would suddenly be all too real.

But then Audrey cried out, "He's breathing!" She fell to her knees at Barnardo's side, shaking his arm first gently and then more aggressively. He didn't stir, but I could see she was right. He wasn't dead yet.

I knelt down beside Miss Snooty Cat and put a hand on her belly. She too was still breathing, but just barely. And she didn't rouse at my touch.

"What happened?" I asked. "Was it the cream or just a coincidence?"

Audrey said nothing, but I could tell she was deep in thought. She picked a careful path on tiptoes around the bodies and spilled cream to the refrigerator. She opened up the fridge, bent forward to dig through the contents, then emerged with a bottle of mineral water.

A green bottle of mineral water. I realized what she was doing even before she popped the cap and started pouring the water out of the bottle.

She was going to do the spell I had taught her to detect poisons.

"Do you remember the words?" I asked as she set the empty bottle on the counter and took out her wand.

"Every one," she said. Then she started chanting a singsong with more confidence than she had shown the first time she'd done it.

We'd both come a long way since that day months before.

She finished the verbal component of the spell and tapped her hand on the mouth of the bottle. The bottle burst into bright green light, filling the room with a kaleidoscope of shades of green forming geometric patterns of light all around us.

We had done this spell once before, searching for poison inside the teashop. That time, we had searched everywhere until I had seen the faintest bit of green glow coming from Audrey's inhaler. I had barely slapped it out of her hand in time.

Just the memory of that near-miss made me shudder in dread every time I thought of it. I had come so close to losing my best friend, and so soon after meeting her.

But this time, we both at once saw the answering glow of green light emanating from every drop of cream around us.

That was a yes. A definite yes. The cream had been poisoned.

But that only meant that all the other questions were about to begin.

CHAPTER

SEVEN

The next half hour or so passed by in a chaotic rush of activity. Once we sent out the alarm, the neighbors rushed to help. The authorities came, and Barnardo was whisked away to the magical hospital that was tucked away under the grounds of the prosaic university on the other side of the river.

He would get the best possible care, but it might not be enough. And there was nothing more Audrey and I could do for him.

Titus Bloom swore to both Audrey and me over and over again to do whatever he could to help out. Anything at all. We only had to ask.

Clearly, he was still feeling bad about the whole mess that happened when I first came to the Square. But I just thanked him and sent him back to his coffeeshop.

Bartholomew Bullen, who ran the Potions & Magical Sundries shop, cast a few poison identifying spells he knew at once, but to his dismay, they didn't reveal any of the common poisons. Which wasn't surprising. Anyone who would sneak into an apartment inside a magical community and poison one of the magical inhabitants there would almost *have* to use an uncommon poison. But we thanked him, and thanked him again when he swore to keep researching in the hopes he could be of some help.

Cressida Cade from the Inanna Salon & Spa was perhaps the most surprising person to pop into the kitchen after the authorities had carried Barnardo out the door on a levitating gurney.

"Cleopatra let you just slip away?" I asked. Since Cleopatra had yet to hire anyone to help out after the death of her employee and Cressida's only coworker, Delilah Dare, I knew she was working long, hard hours.

But I had forgotten that her attitude to that had been one very much of "Cleopatra needs me too much to harass me." I remembered as she just shrugged. "She hasn't been in for days. I've been on my own."

"Doesn't that make you even busier?" Audrey asked. She was probably thinking of her teashop, which she ran all on her own.

But Cressida just shrugged again. "Not if I cull the appointment book down to a level I can manage. My clients prefer if I'm not stressed out and rushing. And I value my clients." Then she finally gave a little smile that was the opposite of her cool, unworried attitude. "This is my lunch break. I just wanted to see if you needed anything. I know you think all three of us detested Barnardo, but for my part, that was never true."

I had worked that out, slowly, the fact that Cressida wasn't quite like the other two members of the Trio. Although I was still a little annoyed that she hadn't worked harder to let people like Barnardo— or me—know, especially when the Trio's mean girl bullying was at its worst.

But all of that had faded away after Delilah had died. I had assumed the two remaining members of the Trio were just too busy running the Inanna Salon & Spa to find new people to mock and make feel self-conscious.

Although if Cleopatra had truly been taking a bunch of days off, she must have had another project.

One that kept her far from the Square.

Cressida headed back to work, and Audrey and I were alone once more.

Alone in Barnardo's kitchen that smelled of spoiling cream.

And with the body of Miss Snooty Cat.

No one, not the authorities or the neighbors, had known what to do with Miss Snooty Cat. She wasn't a familiar, tied to Barnardo by bonds of magic and companionship. But she wasn't an ordinary pet either. There were witches who were veterinarians, but even they would be hard-pressed to treat such a rare creature as a matagot.

Really, there was only one answer.

"I have to take her into the Tower," I said to Audrey. "The Wizard will know what to do."

Audrey nodded, then helped me scoop up Miss Snooty Cat's inert form. She was lighter than I had expected, and her fur was as soft as cashmere. But the way she flopped around in my arms, never rousing, was more than a little distressing.

"I've never been inside the Tower," Audrey said as she let her hand linger as it cradled Miss Snooty Cat's head. "I've not been invited."

"I know," I said. "I'll have to take her alone. But I'll let you know what's going on just as soon as I know anything, okay?"

Audrey just nodded again, like she didn't quite trust herself to speak.

I had been to the Tower many times, but I had never brought myself inside. Steph always came to pick me up before my lessons with him or the Wizard. I knew I had a standing invitation to go inside whenever I wanted or needed to. I just wasn't sure how to make that happen.

But I also knew that the most powerful source of magic for thousands of miles around was the Tower. And the Wizard had once told me the spell tied to that invitation wasn't so much exerting a new effort as stopping the opposite effect.

Basically, everyone was drawn to the Tower. But the Wizard had put powerful wards around the Tower to keep everyone out. The invitation extended to me just counteracted those wards.

Which meant that getting inside the Tower should be the easiest thing in the world.

I had to push aside the thought that this was likely true for actual witches, and not so much for me. I knew now that I *was* a witch. I just wasn't an ordinary kind of witch. My personal magic, the magic of chaos, wasn't just rare. It had been banned everywhere.

No one could teach me how to master it, since no one knew enough about it. But that didn't mean I didn't have power.

On the other hand, chaos was the last thing I needed in that moment. If the normal order of things was to be drawn to the Tower, I needed to flow with that.

The silver bracelet on my wrist gave a subtle little throb. Like it was affirming my thoughts.

I hugged Miss Snooty Cat close to my chest, closed my eyes, and pictured the fireplace in the Wizard's office, deep in the center of the library.

I pictured the way the bookshelves enclosed that space, the assortment of tables cluttered with experiments in various stages of completion, the two battered old chairs drawn close to the cold fireplace. I pictured the cast-iron spiral staircase that led up into the darkness between the heavy timber rafters above, the curve of the gray stone walls that enclosed the entire library.

But more than that, I summoned the memory of the smells of the paper, the faint lichen smell of the stone blocks that formed the walls, the cinder smell that lingered in the fireplace. And the undertone of tuna that always hung in the air.

The Wizard's favorite food was tuna fish sandwiches. Apparently, he had no fear of mercury, as he ate them nearly every day.

I heard a snapping sound behind me, like a log cracking in a fire, and opened my eyes to find I was standing on the carpet in the Wizard's office. I turned to see the remains of a fire burning down in the fireplace behind me. Despite the August heat, the interior of the

Tower was always a touch cold and damp. But why was a fire still burning when there was no one home?

"Why is *she* here?"

I spun around again, although that voice had spoken directly in my mind. It was Houdini, sounding a bit sullen. But when my gaze found him curled up on the chair opposite the Wizard's usual spot, one eye open in that dragon-like way he always employed when disturbed from a nap, he immediately opened both eyes and stood up.

"What's wrong with her?" he asked, leaving sullen behind for real concern.

"She and Barnardo were poisoned," I said. "Are you here because Steph and the Wizard are back?"

"No, I just got impatient," he said. "I can't make heads or tails of that book on my own. But why did you bring her *here*?"

"I didn't know what else to do," I said. "She won't wake up. I don't know how long she's been like this, but I keep getting this feeling like time is running out."

"Urgency and dread?" Houdini asked, sitting up straighter.

"Yeah. How did you know?"

"I felt it too," he said. "I didn't know why. But that's part of why I came here. It felt... safer." Then he narrowed his eyes, peering closely at Miss Snooty Cat's head dangling limply against the side of my arm. "Is it coming from her?"

"Oh. I never thought of that," I said.

But it made sense. She had magic of her own. I knew that was true. But the exact nature of her power was a mystery.

Still, it made sense. She knew she was in trouble, she and Barnardo both. Even comatose as she was, maybe she was still able to call for help.

If only she had done it sooner.

"You should call for Steph," Houdini said. "Steph and the Wizard both. They need to be here."

"I think you're right," I said.

But then I heard the Wizard's voice behind me, saying, "No need. The Tower already summoned me. Let me see the matagot."

I turned towards the fireplace to see the Wizard there, reaching out with both arms to take Miss Snooty Cat. Steph was beside him, looking a little pale. Jumping around the globe in a hurry tended to do that to him.

I gently laid Miss Snooty Cat into the Wizard's arms, then immediately buried myself in Steph's embrace.

"Barnardo is sick as well," I said, my voice muffled against Steph's shoulder.

"Poisoned," Houdini corrected me.

"Yes, I can see," the Wizard said as he gazed down at the matagot in his arms. Then he carried her over to one of his experiment tables. "Stephanos, my kit, please."

"At once," Steph said, giving me one last squeeze before hurrying to assist the Wizard. The Wizard had cleared a space on a table that had been filled with books left open to various illustrations of fungi, but the bag that Steph dug out of a cabinet to bring over to him looked like an old-school doctor's bag.

"I do hope she doesn't die," Houdini said to me. "And not just because she knows secrets about me that she hasn't told me yet. I didn't like her, but this isn't what she deserved, either."

"I know," I said, picking him up to cuddle in my arms. He sounded so despondent, as if he feared he had somehow caused this by wishing Miss Snooty Cat ill. There was no point in arguing against what wasn't remotely a logical impulse, so I just held him tight.

And anyway, I needed the hug as much as he did.

"Do we know the nature of the poison?" the Wizard asked as he passed something that looked like a magnifying glass up and down Miss Snooty Cat's limp body.

"Audrey and I saw it with Agatha's poison detecting spell," I said. "But that just shows whether a poison is present. It doesn't identify the type. Bartholomew tried a few identifying spells he knows, but he couldn't tell what specific poison was used."

"How were they poisoned?" Steph asked. He was looking over the Wizard's shoulder, but whatever they were seeing through the lens of that magnifying glass was too small and too far away for me to see.

"Something was in a bottle of cream they were sharing," I said.

"So they were at home?" Steph asked, looking over at me with alarm.

"Yes. But I don't know for how long," I said. "Houdini, Audrey and I all had these sensations of urgency and dread, but they only started about an hour ago, when we were going to Barnardo's apartment to look for him, anyway. But the cream had clotted after it spilled. I think they were there on the floor for a while. Is calling out to us something a matagot can do?"

"Possibly," the Wizard said. "I will have to speak to a wizard colleague of mine. She is the foremost expert in matagots. Although she leaves her cottage in the south of France even more rarely than I leave the Tower."

"Do you want me to go to her?" Steph asked. He had not yet taken off the many-colored cloak that aided him in teleporting around the world.

"In a moment. I want to know more first," the Wizard said, trading out the magnifying glass for something that looked like a steampunk stethoscope. He listened intently to Miss Snooty Cat's chest. Then her skull. And then the bottoms of her feet.

"Maybe I should go to the hospital downtown and see how Barnardo is doing," I said. Because watching the Wizard work didn't feel remotely like being actually helpful.

"No, there is no need for that," the Wizard said, even as he examined Miss Snooty Cat's claws one by one. "They are already in contact with me. Barnardo is presenting much like our little friend here. He's stable, but not responding to treatment. Without knowing what poison was used, it's difficult to know what steps to take. They are attempting to identify what they've found in his system, but it's a very long process of elimination."

Then he looked up at me, his gaze intent. "You know as well as I, the list of magical poisons is far longer than the list of prosaic ones."

"Most are exceedingly rare," I said. I felt like I had been called on in class. Like I was trying to respond to a question I had not remotely been prepared for.

Luckily, I had always been good at that. Mostly because I had always done the reading. I couldn't practice magic, but I could get the theories behind everything down cold.

Now I closed my eyes and pictured words on a page from a book I had read so long ago. "There are less than a dozen that are in anything like common use."

"Yes, and these symptoms don't match any of those," the Wizard said, as if agreeing with a point I hadn't quite made yet.

"It's going to take days to test for all the rare possibilities," I said.

"Days or weeks," the Wizard said.

"Would having a sample of the cream help?" I asked.

"I can run tests on it while you tend to the matagot," Steph said to the Wizard.

"That's an adequate first step and should be attempted for the sake of thoroughness," the Wizard said as he folded the stethoscope and put it back into the bag.

"But?" I said.

"But the timeline for that runs the same as for the sampling being done from Barnardo's own body. Days or weeks," the Wizard said.

"So, what can we do?" I asked, trying not to sound as helpless as I felt.

"We can let that process run, as I've said," the Wizard said. "Steph, you and Tabitha should go to Barnardo's apartment and get as much of the material as you'll need to run the tests. By the time you've got the first batch set up to run, I'll have my message prepared for you to take to my wizard colleague who studies matagots. You can bring that to her and come back with a response."

"Of course," Steph said. His nod was determined, as was the set of his shoulders, but I knew he was tired already. Another trip across the world and back was really going to leave him wiped out.

Not that he'd thank me for saying so out loud. But the Wizard knew better than I what Steph's limits were. He wouldn't ask for more than Steph could do.

Although he'd absolutely ask for everything up to that point.

"What about you?" I asked the Wizard. "What will you be doing while Steph is in France?"

"I cannot leave this matagot's side, I'm afraid," the Wizard said. "I've already given her a lifeline to my magic. It's her only hope of holding on long enough for us to solve this. She has greater magical power than she gets credit for, but she's still just a tiny thing."

"I will stay with you," Houdini said. I looked down at him in my arms, but I could see by the lift of his chin that he wouldn't be talked out of this.

"If that's what you want," I said, setting him on the ground. He shook his whole body until all of his fur was standing on end, then trotted over to stand by the Wizard's ankle.

"And me?" I finally asked. "Besides getting the sample for Steph, what else is there for me to do?"

I still really wanted to go to the hospital. Someone should be there with Barnardo. Since his father had died, he had no living family members. And with Miss Snooty Cat also ailing, there was no one but Audrey and me to sit with him, to hold his hand, to wait for him to open his eyes again.

But the Wizard was shaking his head as if reading my mind.

"No, that is not where you are most needed, Miss Tabitha," he said. Although I could hear the empathy in his voice. He knew how badly I wanted to be there.

"Where am I needed?" I asked.

"Here, in the Square," he said as he stroked Miss Snooty Cat's head. "Someone here did this. Either someone from here or someone who came here, but it was done here. And finding out who that was will lead us to what they used to do this. Knowing you, that will be faster than any testing of samples we can do."

"That's what I'll do, then," I said, nodding to myself. "I'll figure this out."

I only wished I felt as confident as I sounded. Because, in truth, I had no idea where to even start.

Who on Earth would ever wish Barnardo harm?

CHAPTER

EIGHT

Steph teleported us both back into Barnardo's kitchen. Barnardo and Miss Snooty Cat might both have been removed, but the front of their forms were outlined in the spilled cream clotted on the linoleum. It was a little too much like crime scene chalk, and I flinched away from the sight.

"I can do this on my own if you need me to," Steph said. He had already taken out his wand and was digging through a bag he had slung across his body before we'd left the Tower.

"No, I'm okay," I said. "I mean, if you're going to magic up what you need from the floor, I guess I can't really help with that. But I'm going to check the fridge for anything else that looks like cream. I should've done that before the bottle spell powered down."

"You can always have Audrey do it again if you want to be sure," Steph said. He had taken a fistful of glass test tubes out of his bag and was popping the stoppers out of them one by one and lining them up on the edge of the counter.

"That's true," I said. But I was scanning my memory of the moment after the spell. The cream on the floor had glowed so brightly it had lit up the entire kitchen even more than the bottle

61

that was the spell's focal point. But I was pretty sure I hadn't seen any kind of glow coming from the cupboards or refrigerator or anything in the canisters on the counter.

Of course, all of those had been shut at the time. Maybe it would be worth a second look at some point.

But there was a lot of cream on the floor. And as I watched Steph use his wand to summon it up in long tendrils, I couldn't imagine the number of tests that would consume it all.

Of course, the list of potential poisons was staggeringly long.

I looked in the cupboards and refrigerator while Steph recapped all of those test tubes. But nothing caught my eye.

Then I looked down at the empty glass bottle that was still laying on its side on the kitchen floor. "That didn't come from the Abergavenny's store," I said. Most of us in the Square did our grocery shopping in their little corner store. They made sure to stock whatever particular items we residents preferred, such as my favorite brand of Greek yogurt.

But I had never seen any dairy in their case that came in glass bottles. Let alone a glass bottle with no label on it whatsoever.

"Where would he have gotten this from?" I asked, picking up the bottle to examine it more closely. But the only marking on the glass was a line up the side with cross marks showing the number of ounces at each level. And that was just a ridge in the glass itself, a generic feature of a bottle meant to be used to store liquids. No source location. No expiration date. Nothing that even identified it as being cream.

"That's probably a place to start," Steph said, his voice lifting ever so slightly at the end in the hint of a question.

"I'll probably start with figuring out who was ever in this apartment besides Barnardo and Miss Snooty Cat, but this is another lead to follow if that doesn't turn up anything, for sure," I said.

He gave me a restrained sort of smile, like he wanted to grin at me, but the tone of the day just wouldn't allow for it. But I felt much the same.

There was always a charge I got from investigating things. But it always came with a counter-charge of sadness. Because usually someone had just died.

Although I wasn't feeling much better this time around. No one had died yet. But this time, if I didn't figure out what had happened soon enough, they might die anyway.

And that would be on me.

"I have to get back to the Wizard," Steph said, stepping around the remains of the cream spill to put an arm around me and kiss me briefly on the forehead. "I'm always just a call of my name away."

"I know. Thanks," I said.

"You've got this," he whispered against my hair.

And then he was gone, and I was alone in Barnardo's dark apartment.

I decided to start with opening up the blinds. But before I had even reached the unused dining room, I heard the clatter of something behind me. Someone was deeper in the apartment, deeper than I had ever been.

Despite the fact I had just been making a bunch of noise opening and closing cupboards while chatting with Steph, I tiptoed to the far side of the kitchen and peered down the darkened interior corridor.

I could see a bathroom through the open door on the left, just past a pair of folding doors I assumed to be a linen closet.

But the clattering sound was coming from the farthest door, the one on the right. Being the only room left in the apartment, it had to be Barnardo's bedroom.

I really wished I had a wand to grip, even though as a tool, a wand was largely useless to me. Still, just squeezing my hands into fists did nothing to make me feel braver. But I made do.

Hands in tight fists, I crept down the corridor towards the open door to Barnardo's bedroom.

As I drew closer and the clattering sound continued on, I realized what I was hearing came from one of those computer keyboards, the ones with the really clacky keys. And the stops and starts of the clattering sounded like someone typing something into a computer and then waiting for a response before typing something else.

Not the strangest sound in the universe. But possibly the strangest sound I'd ever heard in the Square. We might all carry around cellphones the same as prosaics did, but computer searches just weren't how we got information.

Then I reached the point where I could see into the bedroom and saw that the corner of the room past the bed was dominated by four different monitors, each showing different information, some with windows of open files and others scrolling data I couldn't read from so far away.

But I recognized the long blonde hair of the woman who was reading them now.

"Audrey?" I called, finally unfisting my hands.

"Hey, Tabitha," she said, sounding distracted.

"You've been here the entire time?" I asked as I stopped tiptoeing and walked across the room like a normal person to get a better look at what she was doing.

"Yeah, there didn't seem much point in opening the teashop back up," she said. Then she leaned forward to type something else into the computer.

"What are you doing?" I asked.

"I figured I'd look around for clues while you were in the Tower," she said, frowning as she studied one of the screens. "I checked the rest of the kitchen for poisons before the spell ran down, by the way."

"You were listening to me and Steph?" I asked.

"I didn't want to interrupt," she said. Although whether she meant she didn't want to interrupt my and Steph's conversation or whatever it was that she was doing, I wasn't sure. I suspected it was a bit of both.

"I'm guessing you didn't find any," I said.

"No," she said, then sat back in the rather expensive-looking office chair to type something else into that clacky keyboard. It was the kind that was split down the middle, the left-hand and right-hand sides angled in a way that was meant to be more ergonomic.

"I had no idea Barnardo spent so much time on a computer," I mused.

"Hm?" Audrey said, sounding distracted again. Then she sat back to properly look at me for the first time. "Oh, yes. Barnardo is what the prosaics call *extremely online.*"

"Seriously?" I asked, sitting down on the edge of the bed. I guess I felt mildly shocked by that knowledge.

"We knew he likes to gossip," Audrey said with a fond gleam to her eye.

"Well, sure, but that was all the doings of people in the magical world, I thought," I said.

"There are forums, even for that," Audrey said. "But more than that. He is on a lot of websites. I mean, *a lot* of websites. He has so many different user names, I doubt anyone else ever knew they were all him."

"Was he making enemies?" I asked.

"I would say he was running about the average amount for the extremely online," Audrey said. "So, yes. But most of those were online enemies. The kind that will jump on anything he posts and instantly argue with it. But the kind that would chase him down in real life? I've been looking through the forums he frequents the most, but I'm not seeing anyone that motivated."

"A couple of suspects to start with would be nice," I said, looking around the room for anything else that might be a clue. But all I saw were so many signs that the bulk of Barnardo's time was spent at that computer. There were no books on the nightstand, no sign of a TV or a laptop where he could watch shows from the bed or even a more comfortable chair than the one Audrey was sitting in.

Which looked comfortable enough to spend all day in. But I just didn't get the vibe that Barnardo had ever pushed that keyboard away to just watch something.

"That's the thing, I think I do have a few," Audrey said. She tapped at the keyboard again, then turned one of the monitors so that it was more directly facing me.

"MacBeth's Marvels?" I said, squinting at the overly ornate font at the top of what was clearly an online store. I scanned down past the smiling picture of a young man who was definitely not Barnardo to rows and rows of products. It was the same image over and over of some sort of brightly colored liquid inside of a stoppered bottle.

But unlike Steph's modernly manufactured test tubes, these all appear to be bottles of hand-blown glass. They were kind of pretty, especially with the brightly colored liquid glowing in the light from whatever the photographer had been shining on them when the photos had been taken.

Yet the sight of them filled me with unease. It was too clear what Barnardo had been selling.

And it was exactly what he shouldn't have been selling.

"Does he claim...?" I started to ask.

But Audrey cut me off. "Yes. Just that, yes."

I leaned closer to the screen. The pink-colored potion was a love potion. So his shop's bestseller was also his worst offense in magical law.

But a quick scan as Audrey nudged the scroll button on the mouse showed a lot of lesser offenses. Potions that would make you thinner. Potions that would make you successful in business. Potions that would give you an athletic edge.

Potions that should never, ever end up in a prosaic's hands. Because any of them knowing about magic, real magic, put all of us in danger.

"This is all highly illegal," I said. As if Audrey didn't know that already.

"He's not even bothering trying to hide it," Audrey said with a sigh. "It's almost like he was super confident he'd never get caught by the magical authorities."

"Well, in all fairness, until today I don't guess he ever has," I said.

"I already searched all the closets. Wherever he keeps his stock before he mails it out to his customers, it's not here," Audrey said.

"So we have no way of knowing which crime he actually committed," I mused. "He is either conning prosaics with fake goods, or he's selling them real things that are absolutely forbidden."

The first crime turned my stomach a little bit, and didn't feel like anything I could ever imagine Barnardo doing.

But the second was a serious crime against the entire magical community. One that came with the most serious of punishments for any perpetrators.

But that really didn't feel like anything I could ever imagine Barnardo doing either.

"Crafting the real things would be tricky. It would require a very highly trained alchemist. Which I don't know if Barnardo was. Without samples, we can only guess," Audrey said. But then she tapped at the keyboard again, and the screen in front of me changed to a series of open files. Copies of emails.

"Customer complaints?" I asked as they kept popping up one on top of the other.

"Customer complaints," Audrey agreed.

But then she added, "And death threats."

NINE

It was at that point that Audrey admitted she had reached the end of what Liam had taught her to do on a computer. Given how far past any point I'd ever even attempted on a computer she'd gone, I could hardly give her a hard time about that.

"Liam could figure out more," Audrey said as she pushed the keyboard tray closed and sat back in the chair.

"No doubt," I agreed. "I guess we don't need all the monitors. But even with just one, this is a lot to carry downstairs to the teashop."

"I mean, Steph did say Liam could come into the Square, didn't he?" Audrey asked almost shyly.

"He's never been up to your apartment, though. Has he?" I asked.

She flushed a deep scarlet, but shook her head.

"He already knows the biggest secrets about this place. And the spelled oath he swore to Steph keeps us all safe, even Houdini. He can't talk about anything he sees here, even if he wanted to. Which we both know he never would."

"I know," she said, not quite meeting my eyes. "It just felt like a step that needed to wait. I know Steph said it was safe to let him inside. And he's already been all over the bookshop, which is the most magical place in the Square besides the Tower."

"Well, not *all over* the bookshop," I said. "Just up to my nook and back. He's never wandered through the stacks."

"Because you told him not to?" Audrey asked.

"Not in so many words," I said grudgingly. Then I got up from the edge of Barnardo's bed to pace the room. "It's like Miss Snooty Cat's call for alarm, isn't it? We're both feeling a reticence about letting Liam in that isn't about our own actual feelings, is it? Or am I crazy?"

"No, I feel it too," she said. "And, yeah, it feels like something coming from outside me. Maybe the Square's protective magic is making us feel this way. I know its magic is designed to make prosaics pass by without noticing us."

"Right," I said. "That protective magic is still working, even though Liam technically has permission to come inside."

"We can haul all this down to the teashop if we have to, but it really would be easier to bring Liam up here," Audrey said.

"Then it's time to let him into the Square," I said.

But we both stood there for a moment more, neither of us wanting to be the first one to move. I was sure Audrey was overcompensating for her own motives. Of course she wanted Liam to move as freely through her world as she could through his. But she didn't want to be the one to make that call.

So I needed to be the one to bring him inside. Not that I was entirely impartial myself. Liam had been a friend of mine slightly longer than Audrey had known either of us. And I had come to rely on his help in my investigations.

But the instant the word "investigation" popped into my mind, it was like I was suddenly free to move. Finding out who had hurt Barnardo was important to everyone in the Square. And the Square wanted to protect its inhabitants.

"Come on," I said to Audrey. "Let's go down to the teashop to meet Liam. He's usually awake about now, right?" Working overnight, he went to bed right after our breakfasts every morning. But that had been nearly eight hours ago.

"Yes, but I'll text him to be sure he hurries," Audrey said, pulling out her phone even as she followed me back out onto the cast-iron balcony outside the apartment door.

We had to walk all the way to the Tower to get to the staircase down to ground level, then all the way back again to reach the doors of the teashop directly below Barnardo's apartment. Then Audrey crossed the room to unlock the door on the prosaic side of the teashop.

For three heartbeats, nothing happened. Then Liam came bursting through the doorway, red-faced from running.

"Another murder?" he got out between gasping breaths.

"Not quite," I said. "We're hoping he pulls through, but without knowing what he was poisoned with, the odds aren't great."

"It's Barnardo," Audrey told him.

"Oh, no," Liam said. We had all been having breakfast together for months now, chatting and trading stories. Liam was as close to Barnardo as Audrey and I were. "Anything I can do, I'll do it."

"We need some help with his computer," I said.

"I can see that he's gotten some death threats, but I can't figure out who they're from. We're hoping you can poke around a little. Get us a name or maybe even an address," Audrey said.

"Sure," Liam said, nodding. He took a few more breaths, then straightened up, recovered from his run and ready to get to work. "Where's his laptop?"

"It's a desktop thing, actually," I said.

"We need to bring you to it," Audrey said.

"Oh," Liam said, still nodding reflexively. Then he seemed to realize all the implications of her statement and said, "oh," again, only far more slowly and with wider eyes.

"Steph said you were free to move around the Square," I said.

"Yeah. It just felt like maybe I shouldn't do that without a good reason," Liam said.

"This is a good reason," I said.

"Yeah. Yeah, I guess it is," he said.

"It's mostly going to look like a normal neighborhood, honestly," Audrey told him. "The most magical thing here is really the bookshop, and you're familiar with that already."

"Sure," Liam said. He was twisting the straps of his backpack in his hands, a gesture that was so reminiscent of Audrey when she was nervous it almost made me smile.

Almost. But Barnardo's time was running out. And we had to get upstairs.

Audrey locked the door Liam had come in through, then the three of us crossed the teashop to the other set of doors. I gave Liam one last look to be sure he was ready, then swung the doors open wide.

Then we were standing on what was frankly a perfectly ordinary tile patio, with white cast-iron tables and chairs arranged into discreet little arrangements, ready for customers who were willing to brave the heat while sipping at iced tea. It was a little Parisian for Minnesota, but not all that odd.

But Liam stood frozen in place, still clutching those backpack straps so tightly his knuckles had gone grayish-white.

I followed his gaze around the perimeter of the Square. The bookshop, clearly seven stories of books plus an apartment and then an attic, dominated the southern side of the Square. He already knew it was bigger here than the three stories it appeared to be from the Minneapolis street outside, but the immensity of seeing it all as opposed to wandering through the heart of it was imposing, I had to admit.

Most of the apartments on the far side of the Square, including the one Audrey had inherited from her grand-aunt Agatha, were obscured from view by the tall walls of the hedge maze that dominated that side of the open plaza. Still, a few of the taller, more house-like constructions on the top floor poked little spires or awnings into view.

But our side of the plaza was equally spellbinding to Liam, even though it was just an ordinary orchard. Tiny pears and apples nestled among the leaves, still too small for eating, although a few of the raspberry and blackberry shrubs were far enough along to attract clouds of bees and wasps.

Then his gaze reached the northeast corner, the one where the Tower stood. And I could see his blue eyes cloud over ever so slightly before his gaze moved on to the apartments that overlooked the alley in the prosaic world.

That magic was still strong, and wanted nothing to do with him. But even I, someone who had an open invitation to enter and leave the Tower at will, still had trouble looking directly at it. It was easier to see its stone form if I looked somewhere else and tried to catch it just at the periphery of my vision.

"We're going up to the second floor," Audrey said, gesturing towards the stairs.

Liam swallowed and nodded, then gripped his pack again before following her across the very edge of the Square.

We passed the moss-covered stone steps that led down to the cellar and catacombs that were the old witch Volumnia's domain. Liam walked closer to that edge to peer down into the shady depths of that stairwell. But he asked no questions, and I offered no information.

Our varied funerary practices were definitely not something I wanted to get into. Not that day.

"Is Miss Snooty Cat very upset?" Liam asked as our steps rang on the cast-iron balcony that led us back to the bookshop end of the Square, to Barnardo's apartment.

"She's in a coma as well," I said. "Steph and the Wizard are trying to help her. And Houdini is there too. He seems to be feeling guilty, and I can't rouse him out of it. Not that I had a lot of time to try. We really need to find out what they were poisoned with as soon as possible."

"And you think the computer will help?" Liam asked.

"If we find out who did this, we'll be able to get the answer of what poison was used from them," I said. "Or so we hope."

"But why was he getting death threats on his computer?" Liam asked.

"He was running a business," Audrey told him. "One that is at best considered unethical and might even by illegal by our standards. We don't know which just yet."

"Someone found out and threatened him?" Liam asked.

We had reached the door to the apartment, which we had left standing just a little ajar. I swung it wider open, then finally got around to opening all the curtains to let the sunlight in as Audrey led Liam back to the computer desk in the bedroom.

I could hear her explaining all we had already figured out about the nature of Barnardo's business as they headed down the corridor, his questions and her answers fading into murmurs as they entered the room.

I had intended to join them while Liam ran his searches, but instead I found myself distracted by the sight of Miss Snooty Cat's luxurious bed set just where the best sunbeam fell through the south-facing dining room window.

Matagots were magical creatures. I knew they only looked like cats, and yet I had no idea what their true form looked like. Maybe once they turned into cats, they couldn't go back.

Miss Snooty Cat had belonged to Barnardo's father first. And while I didn't know the details of that relationship, I knew the general lore about matagots. They can be caught with a lure of food and then carried home. And once there, so long as they were continually given the choicest food and drink, not only would they remain, but they would give their human captor riches.

Only the lore was very clear on one point: eventually, you had to let the matagot go. Because if you didn't, they could use their magic to make your death long and tortuous.

I knew Barnardo's father had recently died from a long illness, but I didn't know what that experience had been like.

And I didn't know why Miss Snooty Cat had chosen to stay after he had passed. With only the lore to go on, it didn't exactly make sense.

But another question also lingered in my mind.

If Miss Snooty Cat could dispense riches, why was Barnardo running scams for money? He liked good food and nice clothing, but not to the point where money could've been a huge issue.

All the furnishings around me were well made, largely antiques that still would've been pricey when they were new. But they had all belonged to his father. Barnardo hadn't changed a thing since moving in. I knew that because he'd told me. His frugal living was a point of pride for him.

But that really didn't fit with his business model at all. Why scam people if money itself was no object?

I had a feeling I wouldn't really know. Not until Barnardo was awake.

And maybe not even then.

TEN

It soon became clear that even with Liam's help, it was going to take some time to pull a list of suspects from the various sources on Barnardo's computer.

"Because those forums are anonymous?" I asked.

"Well, not as much as the users probably think they are," Liam said. "But no. There are just so many different people who were angry with Barnardo. And just because they don't seem murderous in text on a computer screen doesn't clear them."

"But not being in the area in the last few days would," I said. "Can't we just start with people who seem to live around here? I can check up on them, snoop around or ask questions, while you keep collating your list."

"I did see a name you could start with," Liam said, leaning forward to click through some of the many windows that were open on the four monitor screens. "Then I'll do my thing and hopefully have a few more before you get back. Unless there's a magical way to do this faster?"

He glanced away from the monitors to give me a quizzical look.

"Not that I know of," I said. "Computers weren't really a part of any academy's curriculum when I was in school. Even though nearly all of us have cellphones these days."

"They probably should be," Audrey said.

"You've been spending more time with computers lately than I ever had," I said to her. "You would be more likely to figure something helpful out than I would."

She flushed a deep shade of pink, but quickly shook her head. "No, really, I barely know how to use the things, let alone how they actually work. But with your talent for languages, I just know you'd get further than I have if you just poked around one a little bit."

All I could think of was the blue screen of death. I had fried my uncles' bookshop computer the first time I had touched it. And I was still paranoid every time I needed to use the new one that I was going to do it again. Even though, with my silver bracelet, my chaos energy wasn't flaring up like that anymore.

"Computer science and math go together great," Liam said as he tapped one final key. We all heard the whirring sound of a different machine waking up and starting to run, but it took the three of us together to find the printer inside of a closed cabinet behind the closet door.

Liam took the printed pages out of the printer's tray and glanced at them before handing them to me. But I took them without looking at them. "What do you mean about math? Did Steph tell you something?" I asked.

"Steph? No, I haven't seen Steph in days," Liam said. But his ears, not quite hidden by the blond curls that really needed a trim, were a brilliant shade of scarlet.

"My brother," I guessed.

So he had seen the books I had left out on the table in my nook in the bookshop. Great.

"He was just surprised you hadn't studied the higher levels of math and their magical implications before," Liam said. "I mean, given how you've studied just about everything else."

"Did he also mention that higher levels of math are pretty much exclusively the domain of the most elite of ritual magicians?" I shot back. Because I had always known that path was closed to me. No one had any use for a ritual magician who couldn't perform a ritual.

"Yes, actually," Liam said, still blushing furiously. "I think that's what surprised him. That you weren't as deeply versed in that as you are in everything else."

I chewed at my lip, wondering just what *that* meant. Liam sounded like he'd taken it as a compliment directed towards me. And I could see how he would interpret it that way.

But it could also mean Mercutio was probing him for hints of my weaknesses. And not being versed in his own brand of magic would be a huge weakness.

If he was a threat. Which I still wasn't sure about.

"If you'd prefer that I didn't discuss you at all with him, I totally understand," Liam said all in a rush. "I just thought, anything that brought the two of you closer together."

"He should be talking to her himself if he wants to be closer with her," Audrey said to him.

"I know," Liam said. But he was looking at me anxiously, waiting for me to say something.

"It's okay," I told him. "You don't have to shut him down if he has questions. I mean, you know what the secrets are that you can't divulge. I'm officially telling you everything else you want to share is fair game. I don't want to make things weird between you and your roommate."

"He's just curious about you," Liam said. "But also, I think he finds you intimidating."

"Me? Intimidating?" I said, flabbergasted. "He's a ritual magi-cian, even if an unemployed one. I work in a bookshop, and I'm kind of under-qualified even for that."

"You are not," Audrey said, punching me lightly in the arm.

"Well, still. Maybe Steph intimidates him, but not me," I said.

"No, it's definitely you," Liam said. "I think he wants to have a better sense of his footing with you before he opens up. Not that I'm any expert in emotions or anything."

"No, you do read people pretty well, actually," I said. Then I finally looked down at the paper in my hand. "So this guy. Troy McFarland."

"He ordered a really staggeringly large amount of the love potion from Barnardo about a month ago," Liam said. "Barnardo emailed him specifically to verify the amount. And he clarified that the potion was designed for the customer to drink to be more receptive to possible connections with others. Definitely not for the customer to put into other people's drinks to make them fall in love with the customer."

"But he bought a whole case, anyway?" Audrey asked.

"Two cases," Liam said. "He told Barnardo he understood the instructions on its proper use, and then sent a complaint every time he had failed to pick up any women when he was out clubbing."

"At least he was drinking it himself like he was supposed to," I said. Although glancing at the printout of their email exchanges only made the whole question of what Barnardo had been doing exactly that much more confusing.

Creating a potion that made the drinker more receptive to connections with others wasn't illegal or even amoral in the magical world. Although I was a little curious if it worked, and if it did, *how* it worked.

My chemistry skills were stronger than my calculus skills, and especially since I had started working on spells with Audrey, my potion skills were top-notch. Or, at least, my understanding of the formulas for the potions. I still couldn't mix one myself to save my life.

But the idea of Barnardo selling anything in any way magical to prosaics? Even if they used it as intended, that was still very much against the rules. Secrecy was always our first and last rule.

But Liam was shifting his weight from foot to foot, and I knew before he spoke his answer that the words were making him uncomfortable, just relating them to me.

"He gave it to women," I guessed with a frustrated sigh.

But to my surprise, Audrey laughed out loud.

Liam and I both turned to her, mouths hanging agape.

"Sorry," she said, waving our looks away. "It's just... if this potion did what Barnardo said, and he was giving it to women in random clubs and bars? These women would've been receptive to the people around them they were most likely to connect with."

Then Liam laughed out loud. "Oh, right. Definitely not *this* guy."

"Definitely not this guy," I agreed. "That explains the increasingly irate emails."

"Barnardo refused to refund his money. And Troy threatened to sue," Liam said.

"Which would be tricky, since Barnardo doesn't really exist in his world," I said.

"Barnardo doesn't, but MacBeth's Marvels does," Liam said. "All the business paperwork is filed and correct. He even charges sales tax correctly, and the business pays all the proper state and federal taxes."

"Okay, Audrey and I will go chat with Troy, see where he's been the last few days. Although I don't know how a prosaic could've gotten into the Square to poison Barnardo and Miss Snooty Cat. Or how he got a hold of a poison that seems pretty clearly magical," I said.

"MacBeth's Marvels might not be the first or only place he's ordered magical items from," Audrey pointed out.

"Something else we can ask him, for sure," I said.

"I think most of the other customers I can eliminate just because they live in different states or countries, but I'll double check," Liam said, already heading back to the computer desk. "Then I'll dig into his online interactions. Maybe this doesn't have anything to do with his business at all."

"Maybe," I said. But my gut didn't believe it.

Selling magical potions and then nearly dying from a magical poison just felt too related. Trolling on Internet forums? Not so much.

"Troy's address is on the original order on the first page I printed for you," Liam said. "He lives in a condo right by the river. Maybe even overlooking the river. But I know the block his street number is on. There's nothing cheap on that stretch of road."

"Thanks, Liam," I said, folding the pages and tucking them into my back pocket.

Audrey gave Liam a quick kiss on the cheek, and then the two of us headed back to her teashop.

"We can do this after closing time if you'd rather?" I said, feeling a little guilty that she was losing money even as we ran around trying to solve yet another crime. Her business was doing better than it had when her grandaunt Agatha had run it, but I knew her profits were still barely more than her expenses.

"No, I want to find who did this to Barnardo," Audrey said. "He might not have much time. And if I made you wait a few hours so I could sell a few more iced teas..."

"He would absolutely understand and not blame you at all," I said. But I knew she'd blame herself, so I didn't argue when we merely passed in one door and then out the other, emerging into the prosaic streets of Minneapolis.

"This way, I think," I said. I knew which way took us closer to the river, anyway. But even as we walked, I dug out my cellphone to get us the rest of the way to the correct address.

We reached the last street before the river itself, then turned to walk along a tree-lined sidewalk until we reached an old stone and brick building that had once been some sort of mill but was now split into condos.

"He's on the first floor," I said, squinting at the house number on the printout one last time before stuffing it back in my pocket. "So he doesn't overlook the river."

"Nice view of the park across the street, though," Audrey said. "Should we knock?"

I nodded, then climbed the three steps up the truncated front porch to knock on the door. Then I rang the bell. And then I knocked again.

"It is kind of early in the afternoon," Audrey said. "Maybe he's not home from work yet."

"Should we wait at that café over there, do you think?" I asked.

Before Audrey could answer, another voice spoke from behind me.

"Well, this is a delight. Although I don't remember ordering two lovely ladies to be delivered to my doorstep."

I turned to see a man standing behind me, a messenger bag slung over one shoulder, a tall cup of some sort of icy beverage in the other. He looked to be about thirty, maybe a little past it, but fit and dressed towards the nicer end of "business casual."

And although his words had been directed towards both of us, he had his eyes glued on Audrey. I could tell it was making her nervous, because she was already tucking her hair back behind her ears.

I took half a step towards him, sharp words at the ready to drag his attention back from his ridiculously obvious perusal of Audrey from head to toe.

But it was only half a step, and no words emerged, because I felt a sudden intense pressure on my mind. A pressure I had felt before while investigating a different crime in Vienna.

The pressure was gone as quickly as it had come, but it left me feeling cold and shaky. My skin was still covered with the sweat I had worked up on the walk over, but my flesh was all clammy now, and my teeth were nearly chattering.

This feeling had been familiar then, although I still didn't quite know why. I had never learned where it had come from.

But it had found me again on the other side of the world. Close to home. And I really didn't like any of the things that could bode at all.

CHAPTER

ELEVEN

My hearing had gone all muffled, like I was standing underwater listening to a conversation happening on the pool deck. But I eventually looked up to realize that a visibly distraught Audrey had been calling my name over and over again. And even Troy had a worried look to him. Although I was sure he was just preoccupied with the thought of what attention a strange young woman collapsing on his doorstep might draw.

"You should bring her inside," he said to Audrey.

"No. I'm all right," I said, even as Audrey caught my elbow.

"You look like you're about to faint," she whispered to me.

"It's done now," I said. But I didn't pull my arm out of her grasp. I kind of needed her support, especially as I squinted my eyes against the August sun to peer at the buildings around us.

The pressure was gone now, but it had come from someone. It had come from somewhere. And it felt like it had come from somewhere close. Like someone was still watching me.

It might come again.

"At least come in for a glass of water," Troy said. He had already unlocked his front door and was waving for Audrey to bring me inside.

"No, I'm okay," I said, and forced my spine to straighten up. I was starting to feel the heat of that sun beating down on me again, and the clammy feeling was passing.

Audrey released my arm, but I could see she was torn between worry for me leading to a desire to sit me down in a shady place with a cold drink, and a revulsion at the idea of going inside the darkened apartment of the man who was making no attempt to hide his leering at her.

It wasn't hard to see why this man kept striking out with women. He was a lot.

And I really didn't appreciate him not seeming to get how disturbing his behavior was to Audrey.

I mustered up my brightest smile as I turned more fully towards him. And also stepped into the line of sight between him and Audrey. Although, again, he didn't bother pretending like he wasn't trying to look past me. I adjusted my glasses and crossed my arms, waiting for his attention to come back to me.

His thick brown hair was swept back in a look I was sure had been much more slicked down when he'd left the house that morning, but humidity and the natural thickness of his hair were conspiring to lift it into something closer to a pompadour.

As if he felt my eyes on that hair, he hiked the bag strap up a little higher on his shoulder, then ran a hand over that hair. It laid down nicely. For about two seconds.

He licked his lips slowly, his eyes still on Audrey, and I just knew whatever he was going to say next, she didn't want to hear it.

It was time for me to take the initiative.

"Troy McFarland?" I said, still projecting bright energy.

"That's right," he said, not quite glancing at me. "Is there something I can help you with?"

"We were hoping you could answer a few questions for us," I said.

"I'd love to," he said. "But let's step inside where it's cooler."

"Oh, that's not necessary," Audrey said at once. "We can talk out here."

"With all this traffic?" he said. Behind him, a car was indeed passing by. But it was an electric car, its motor barely making a hum, the tires crunching over a few fallen twigs from one of the trees with a soft snap.

"Maybe we can step over to that café," I offered.

"I already have an iced coffee. I don't need another," he said to me. His tone wasn't quite nasty, but it was definitely testy.

Then he fixed his attention back on Audrey. "Everything on their menu is terribly watered down even before they pile in the ice. Why don't you come inside and I'll make you something refreshing, and then you can ask whatever you like. I bet you're an Arnold Palmer girl. Am I right?"

Which was a spot-on guess. Audrey loved Arnold Palmers.

And he was grinning at her, and to be honest, he *did* have a really charming smile when he put the leering on pause. It sparkled in his eyes and looked so genuine.

No one would ever guess he had just snapped at me the second before.

Well, anyone who hadn't been standing there when it happened. Like Audrey had.

"Listen," I said to Troy. And then stopped.

My plan to walk over to his condo and ask him a few questions had suddenly developed a glaring flaw. Or rather, I had suddenly seen that the flaw had always been there.

We weren't in the Square, where everyone knew who I was. They might not want to answer my questions, but they weren't going to question my right to ask them.

But I could suddenly see from Troy's point of view, two women showing up on his doorstep to ask him about his dealings with an online business, dealings that should technically have remained private, was going to be more than a little suspicious.

"Listen," I said, more loudly this time as his attention had shifted back to putting Audrey under uncomfortable levels of scrutiny. "Audrey and I are trying to find other customers of a business who might be unhappy with the service they were provided. For..." I fought for the prosaic words I had heard in fictional contexts before, if never part of my own real world. "Legal... something," I finished lamely.

"Class action lawsuit," Audrey said.

"Oh, yeah?" Troy said, mildly interested. And apparently not thinking anything in particular about the stilted way Audrey had said those words. Like she was speaking a line of foreign dialogue she didn't understand and had learned phonetically.

"Right," I said, crossing my arms more tightly and nodding in a way that I hoped exuded confidence.

"What's the business? Not that café," he said, shifting his gaze suspiciously towards the café in question.

"No, not the café," I said. "It's an online establishment. A magical store."

"Allegedly," Audrey put in.

"Alleged magical store," Troy repeated, as if he thought we were both nuts. But then understanding dawned on him. "Oh, you mean MacBeth's Marvels, don't you? You know they're local?"

"We do now," I said. "I had a friend hack into their website so we could find the name of other customers. Like you."

And that wasn't even entirely a lie.

"We don't have to know what anyone ordered or why they wanted it," Audrey said in a rush. "The important thing is, nothing did what it was claimed to do. Was that your experience, too?"

"Definitely," he said, hiking the strap of that bag up onto his shoulder again. "A class action lawsuit. Shouldn't that involve lawyers?"

"Eventually," I said, still hoping I sounded like I knew what I was talking about.

But from his almost condescending look, I knew I hadn't sold it.

Luckily, not for the reason I feared.

"You girls are awfully young," he said, looking from me to Audrey and back again. And then back to Audrey, more lingeringly. "Do you even know what you're doing? Lawsuits aren't for the fainthearted."

"We're figuring it out as we go," I said.

But he was still looking at Audrey. Who was still tucking her hair behind her ears, over and over. And it was more than the heat from the sun making her skin so pink.

Still, before I could intervene, she looked directly at him with a cold intensity that made even me want to take a step away from her. "It's more than a matter of the thing that I bought not doing what was promised."

"Were you hurt?" he asked.

She hugged herself and nodded, but that sense of tightly wound yet cold intensity never left her.

He chewed at the end of the straw in his no longer icy drink, but his gaze on Audrey was no longer a leering one. No, now all I sensed in him was a greedy interest.

Indeed, when his inner ruminations finished, he said briskly, "It's a good thing you both found me. I'm in an ideal position to be all sorts of help to you in this matter. I've kept an extensive record of my own correspondence with that company, as well as a log of my own uses of the product I purchased. I was on the verge of contacting a lawyer myself. But you say you've actually been *hurt* by what you took?"

"I don't really want to go into details about it," Audrey said, still hugging herself. "It's private."

"Sure, sure," Troy quickly assured her. Then he turned to set his bag just inside the door of his apartment.

His back was turned to us only for a moment, but that was long enough for Audrey to wink at me and give me a quick grin before resuming her cold, self-hugging victim stance.

She was quite the actor. I had to work hard to smother my answering grin. Not that Troy was looking at me at all.

"This really isn't the kind of conversation we should be having on a sidewalk," he said. "Why don't you come inside? The offer of a cold drink still stands. For both of you," he added with almost a glance my way. Then he came back down the stairs to reach for one of Audrey's tightly crossed arms.

"No, I think here is fine," Audrey said. And she tried to take a step away from him.

"Come on. Don't be like that," he said, and reached out again to try to catch her arm.

He never actually touched her.

But only because the moment I saw the look of alarm on Audrey's face when he reached out to grab her, something just exploded out of me.

I didn't have a momentary conversation with my silver charmed bracelet asking me if I wanted access to my full power. I didn't have a sense of my power starting to spark up. I had no warning at all.

I just had a split-second urge to intercede in whatever was about to happen, to protect my friend.

But instead of grabbing that guy's arm, I guess I kind of... knocked him unconscious?

I mean, one second I was reaching out to him, and the next a wave of force rippled out of me like a tsunami.

And then Audrey and I were standing on the sidewalk looking down at an unconscious man whose front was quickly getting soaked by the contents of his now-spilled iced coffee.

CHAPTER

TWELVE

We both stood there, looking down at the unconscious figure between us for way too long.

"Um, Tabitha?" Audrey said, barely more than a whisper. "I don't think he's waking up."

"I think he's getting a nosebleed," I said.

He was definitely getting a nosebleed. It wasn't even subtle.

But I guessed that meant he wasn't dead.

"We should get him inside," Audrey said.

"You want to drag him up three steps?" I asked. He wasn't a particularly big man, but that was still a lot of floppy, dead weight to haul up a stoop while in a hurry not to be seen.

"I can hover him a little, but we have to at least make it look like we're moving him," Audrey said.

I fought back the sudden urge to break into hysterical laughter. The idea that getting caught moving a man I had just knocked unconscious would be okay so long as it looked like we were doing it with our muscles and not with magic was... well, laughable.

"Tabitha," Audrey said in what was basically a mom voice I

91

didn't even know she had. But it snapped me out of it. I ran to take my position at his shoulders as Audrey was whispering the words of a simple levitation spell while grasping his calves.

Troy McFarland wasn't exactly weightless, even with the spell, but he was light enough for the two of us to maneuver him up the stairs and into his own living room. Audrey kicked the door shut behind her, then we got his inert body over to the couch before the last of her spell faded away and he fell onto the leather cushions with all his full weight.

Audrey looked down at him with deep annoyance.

Then she looked up at me with, if anything, even more annoyance.

"Sorry?" I said. "I don't know what happened. I just didn't want him to touch you."

"I thought I made it clear to you that I was acting a part. I wasn't that upset," she seethed.

I bit my lip, but didn't speak my own thoughts. Still, I was pretty sure she had been acting like she didn't want that man touching her because she really *didn't* want that man touching her.

Audrey must have guessed my thoughts anyway, because she sighed in a frustrated sort of way, then said, "I'm sure you meant well, but I'm not some delicate creature that can't stand to be touched by strangers. Even unwelcome touches. I can deal with it on my own, okay?" Her self-hug was gone now. The folding of her arms was a more aggressive posture, ensuring that her body language fully backed up the glower she was sending my way.

"I know," I said. "I didn't mean... I don't know what happened."

Which was all too true. Although I couldn't help feeling like whatever had put that pressure sensation on my mind minutes before had to be involved somehow.

"It wasn't your usual brand of chaos," Audrey allowed. "I guess that's a good thing. That kind of pyrotechnics in this neighborhood?"

"I don't think anyone saw anything," I said. "Whatever came out of me, at least it was quiet."

"It *was* quiet," Audrey said. Grudgingly.

"His nose has stopped bleeding," I said. "And I can see his chest moving. He seems okay. Maybe he'll just wake up in a minute or two."

"I'm not leaving him unattended, if that's what you mean," Audrey said.

"No, of course not," I said. "We didn't even get to ask him any questions."

"Isn't it weird that he didn't seem to even care what we wanted to ask him about? I mean, it felt a little too trusting, how quickly he wanted us to come inside his place," Audrey said, finally letting go of her annoyance with me to turn her attention back to Troy.

"I thought it was just me being paranoid," I said. "There was a bit of greed in him at the idea of joining in a lawsuit. But even before that, he seemed awfully eager to get us inside and offer us something to drink. Well, *you*, anyway."

"I wonder if he had any of Barnardo's love potion left? Or maybe something else, something he bought from a less ethical source?" Audrey said.

"Wouldn't even have to be magical," I said. "There are prosaic things that can be a lot more awful than what Barnardo was selling."

I started to look around the condo, taking in the sparse furnishings. Troy seemed to prefer fewer but pricer items. Which would make searching for clues easier.

But Audrey was still looking down at Troy himself. "He's going to be pretty angry when he wakes up, I think."

"And confused," I said.

"I think angry first," Audrey said.

"Do you want to tie him up?" I asked.

Audrey was hugging herself tightly again. But this time, she looked like she was really cold. The air conditioning was on a bit too high, leaving the shadowy condo interior almost frigid. "I just want to go," she said. But then she sighed. "But that doesn't help Barnardo, does it?"

"One of us should watch him and the other one look around," I said. There was an easy chair angled on the other side of the coffee table from the couch, and draped over the back of the chair was a purple and gold fleece blanket. I picked it up and held it out for Audrey. "I'll look if you want to stay here."

"Okay," Audrey said, taking the blanket and wrapping it around her shoulders. She took out her wand before perching on the arm of the easy chair, close enough to watch Troy's face for signs of waking, but out of his arm's reach if he should wake up in a hurry.

There was nothing in the living room besides the couch, coffee table, and easy chair, and nothing on the coffee table looked anything like a clue. So I headed into the tidy little kitchen and started opening cupboards.

I didn't get the impression that Troy cooked much. There were a few bottles of condiments in the fridge along with the remains of three different takeout meals, but the cupboards didn't hold much besides an array of coffee cups and travel mugs.

I went back into the living room and then past Audrey to the other end of the condo. The bathroom had a single cabinet which held two bottles I recognized as Barnardo's love potion, although neither had been opened. I put them in my pockets. They weren't meant to be in the prosaic world in the first place, and since we hadn't found any sign of stock in Barnardo's apartment, having samples of just what he had been selling might be important at some point.

But when my eyes made a last pass over the array of mouthwash, lotions and creams, I spotted another glass bottle shoved to the back of the crowded space. The liquid inside wasn't pink like the love potion. It was green. I turned it over in my hand to read the label.

It was a confidence-building potion. Ironic, really. If there was anything Troy McFarland lacked, it wasn't confidence. He had been very sure that Audrey would respond to him. I had even gotten the vibe that he was confident he could make me disappear if he wanted me to. That I was on the verge of accepting his suggestion that I go wait for Audrey somewhere else until they were done talking.

No, he definitely had no lack of confidence.

I put that bottle in my pockets with the others.

I peered into the trash, but just like the same receptacle in the kitchen, there was nothing in it. If he'd consumed the contents of any of Barnardo's potions, there was no sign of it now.

I made a quick search of his bedroom, but like his living room, it was so sparse it didn't take much time to complete my sweep. The stand beside his bed had no drawers, and there was nothing under the bed. The single dresser had three drawers holding nothing but clothing, and his closet had nothing but clothes and shoes.

It was weird. Did the man have no hobbies? But there was no sign of sports or gaming equipment, of music or books, nothing.

I was almost feeling sorry for him as I came back out into the living room, where Audrey was still studying his face with unwavering intensity.

"I think he has a computer in that bag of his," I said. "Do you want to check it out while I watch him?"

Audrey didn't say anything. She just pushed away from the chair, keeping the fleece blanket around her shoulders, and knelt at the coffee table as I took out the laptop and set it in front of her.

"Maybe that's useless," I said as I took her spot sitting on the easy chair's arm. "Don't those things have passwords?"

Audrey said nothing. She just reached over to grab Troy's right hand and pressed his fingertip to the power key. The screen switched from the lock screen to his desktop, and she set to work.

"I can see his side of the correspondence we already have," she said as she tapped away at the keyboard. "He kept it all in a folder. Maybe he was serious about suing, but honestly, this guy just seems very neat and organized."

"Maybe a little too neat and organized," I mumbled. There wasn't even any art on his walls. They were just unrelentingly beige.

"Oh," Audrey said. Just a short little syllable, and yet I knew at once that whatever she had seen was deeply worrying.

"We can go back to the tie him up plan," I said, sitting forward on the chair arm.

"No, I think we're safe," she said. But her frown only deepened as she worked at the computer. "I'm going through his internet history. He didn't know who Barnardo really was or where he lived. MacBeth's Marvels only lists a PO Box and an email address, not enough for this guy to go on. But he was definitely trying to find him."

"You're sure he didn't succeed?" I asked.

"No, I don't think so," Audrey said. "He was researching private investigators, but judging from the emails he exchanged with three of them, he considered them all too expensive for what he wanted."

"Not murderous revenge, then," I said. "That is usually more of a 'money's no object' kind of thing."

"I don't see any internet history that ties him to any of Barnardo's online presences," Audrey said. Then she shut the laptop lid with a sigh. "The prosaic police could trace his phone and know if he was anywhere near the Square in the last few days, but that's not something we can do on our own, I don't think."

"Do the poison spell again," I suggested, pushing away from the easy chair to rush over to the fridge. There was a bottle of salad dressing in green glass in the door. I poured the last of the contents into the sink and rinsed it out before bringing it to Audrey.

"I'm getting to be an old hand at this," she said with a half-smile. Then she spoke the words of the spell. Soon, the darkened condo interior was filled with dancing kaleidoscopic colors.

But nothing was catching that glow. I opened every cabinet in the kitchen and bathroom and even opened the dresser drawers in the bedroom again, but nothing.

"Nothing," I said as I walked back into the living room where Audrey was frowning down at Troy once more. "It was a long shot, anyway. Well, hopefully Liam has something more for us by the time we get back."

"We can't leave him like this," Audrey said. "The nosebleed might have stopped, and his breathing might look like he's just sleeping, but we don't *know* that he's okay."

"No, I agree," I said. "I don't know what I did to him, but I really think he should've opened his eyes by now."

I grabbed his shoulders and gave him a little shake, then a more vigorous one. I kind of wanted to slap him, but before I had even quite raised up an arm, Audrey was shaking her head at me with that mom sternness again.

"Every spell has a counter spell," I murmured to myself. An old axiom from my school days, although one that had been the topic of many a debate.

Not that it mattered. Even if it were universally true, I couldn't craft a counter spell to an unknown spell. And I had no idea what it had been that had rushed out of me.

There had been no words. There had been no gestures. And I had never in my life used a wand.

It hadn't been a spell so much as raw magic. But even with all my recent training with Steph and the Wizard, I still understood all too little about my raw magic.

"Tabitha?" Audrey asked. She was starting to sound really concerned.

Not that I could blame her. Troy might have been a borderline creep, maybe even more than borderline if he had gotten enough time to do whatever he had been planning.

But whatever was happening to him now was definitely overkill.

"I can't fix this," I said. "But I know someone who probably can."

I really didn't want to fall into the habit of calling him every time I messed up. Because it was embarrassing. Because it wasn't fair to him. Because it wasn't what I wanted our relationship to be about, at all.

But mostly because it was embarrassing.

And yet, I really had no idea how to fix whatever had happened to Troy McFarland.

So I took a deep breath, braced myself mentally, and said in a tremulous voice, "Steph?"

And just like that, he was there, almost as if he'd been there the entire time, standing just behind Audrey's shoulder and looking, as she did, down at Troy.

"Well, this is certainly not what I was expecting," he said.

CHAPTER

THIRTEEN

I tried to tell Steph everything that had happened, but I wasn't sure if I made a lot of sense. I knew I was babbling, and telling things out of order. And also pacing and gesturing a lot.

Any hope I might have held that Audrey would jump in and help went pretty quickly out the window. I wouldn't say she looked like she was in shock, exactly. But she definitely looked like she knew we had gotten in over our heads and was withdrawing to her own inner ruminations.

But Steph listened until my ranting finally wound down, never interrupting or trying to get me to slow down my anxious pacing.

And when I had fallen silent, he remained quiet himself, tugging at his lip as he mulled something over.

Then he said, "And you're sure what you felt outside was the same thing as you felt in Geneva?"

Audrey snapped out of her reverie to look up at him and ask, "That's what we're starting with?" Then she gestured at the unconscious man we were all gathered around but not looking at.

"He's fine," Steph said with an offhand wave. "But the pressure on your mind, that was definitely familiar?"

"Yes," I said. "But it was only there for a minute. Not even, probably only twenty seconds or so. And then it was gone, and I didn't sense anyone still around us."

"I wouldn't expect that you would," Steph said with an almost apologetic look to me. "Sorry, but you've not been trained for that sort of thing. I think we're dealing with a very powerful wizard who has chosen twice to reveal themselves to you."

"Why?" Audrey asked.

"That I really wish we knew," Steph said.

"Is it dangerous here?" Audrey asked, hugging herself again.

"I don't think so," he said, although if he'd done anything like magically scanning the area, I had seen no sign of it.

"It feels dangerous," I said. "Someone found me in Geneva, and now they've found me here. Only I actually live here. I don't like it."

"Nor do I," Steph said gravely. Then he finally looked down at Troy sprawled across the couch. He picked up one limp arm by the wrist like a nurse taking a patient's pulse. Then he let it drop to instead touch Troy's face with both hands and gently peel back his eyelids.

The sight of the whites of Troy's rolled-back eyes made me suddenly squeamish, and I shuddered as I looked away.

"I don't know how I even did this," I admitted.

"No, what you described doesn't sound like your usual magic," Steph said. He stepped back from Troy and pulled at his own lip again. "How much like the pressure on your mind did it feel? Was it familiar but unplaceable, like that?"

"It was totally alien," I said. "It was like something I've never felt before just rushing through me. Then it was gone, and he was out cold."

"You were trying to protect me," Audrey said.

"But when I feel threatened, I set things on fire," I said. Then I felt my cheeks flush hotly as I added, "Not on *purpose*. But that's what usually happens."

"I don't recognize the magic that did this, but I shouldn't have any trouble pulling him back," Steph said.

"That's a relief," Audrey said. "I was afraid this was going to be permanent, or would mean taking him to a prosaic hospital. Or worse, one of ours."

"No, he'll be right as rain in a moment," Steph said. "But I'm going to have a bit of a talk with him when he's awake. Just the two of us."

"About the case?" I asked.

"Do you have more questions for him?" he asked.

"Not really," I said. "I just meant, what else is there for you to discuss with him?"

"Respect for women?" Audrey said with a raised eyebrow.

"I can't teach him that in one conversation," Steph said. Then smirked as he added, "Not ethically, anyway."

"So?" I asked, lifting my hands.

"I need to know what he thinks happened, and make sure his memories aren't anything that need to be modified," Steph said. "I like to have as light a touch as possible when I'm working with a prosaic who's seen too much. But I still have to be sure he doesn't bring trouble to the Square."

"You're going to wipe his memories?" Audrey asked.

"Only if absolutely necessary," Steph said. "After the whammy Tabitha put on him, there's a good chance he doesn't even remember the last hour or so. In that case, all I have to do is slip out unobtrusively. But if he does remember talking to the two of you, in the first few moments after waking I can still feed him enough false information that he'll just modify his own memory with no need for me to use any magic."

"That really works?" Audrey asked.

"The mind is susceptible in such states," Steph said. "Also, frankly, most prosaics are happier with simple explanations that don't involve changing their entire worldview to include magic in it."

"He might not be one of those, though," I said. "He's been shopping from at least Barnardo and possibly other magicians who sell things to prosaics. He's at least open to the possibility that that stuff works."

"Noted," Steph said.

"I guess you want us to go so we don't interfere in that process then," Audrey said with a sigh.

"He might remember you even without seeing you again, but the odds of him forgetting entirely are higher if you're not here when he wakes up," Steph agreed.

"Maybe Liam has another lead for us by now," she said to me.

"Before you dig into that," Steph said before I could speak, "Tabitha, you really need to go see the Wizard."

"Has something happened?" I asked, anxiety suddenly flooding my entire body like pins and needles. "Is Barnardo okay?"

"Barnardo is the same, the last I heard," Steph said. "No, you need to tell him what you just told me."

"About that pressure feeling like in Geneva?" I asked. Even I could hear the inappropriately hopeful tone in my voice as I asked that question.

"Yes, but also about what you did to Troy here," Steph said, not quite chidingly.

"She felt threatened, she said," Audrey said, once more rising to my defense.

"I felt like *you* were threatened," I clarified.

"That's not the issue," Steph said. "The power that flowed through you wasn't *of* you, was it?"

"Wasn't it?" I asked, suddenly confused.

"Are you saying someone used Tabitha as a conduit to attack Troy? For hitting on me? Why?" Audrey asked.

"The cause and effect might not be that clear-cut, and it's always possible this is some wildly improbable coincidence," Steph said. "But wizards with good intentions don't announce their presence with vague sensations on the mind. They come out and say hello.

And that's twice this particular wizard has let you know they were there without coming out to say hello."

"Do you think this same wizard is the one who knocked out Troy?" Audrey asked.

"I don't know," Steph said. "That's why I want you to talk to the Wizard about it. He might not know either, but he should definitely be kept up to date with these developments."

"I would feel safer knowing he knew," I admitted. Although the idea of going to the Wizard to tell him I knocked a prosaic unconscious, even if by accident or sort of in self-defense, felt a lot like going to the principal's office.

Only this time, without the fire damage I would have to apologize for.

"You're sure he's going to be okay?" I asked as Steph guided Audrey and me to the door to let us back out into the still-hot August afternoon.

"He'll be fine," he said. "Hopefully he remembers just enough to keep his hands to himself in the future, but no promises."

"Let us know if he seems like a murderous poisoner," Audrey said.

If it was an attempt at a joke, none of us so much as smiled. Steph just nodded, then gestured us to go outside so he could shut the door behind us.

"I'm sorry," I said to Audrey as we started the walk back to the Square.

"For what?" she asked.

"That didn't go the way I thought it would," I said.

"I don't think I was ever in any actual danger," Audrey said. "And I can handle being uncomfortable. I mean, we knew we were going to talk to him because he was someone we suspected of *murder*, right? Being uncomfortable is sort of the least I was worrying about."

"I might have put the entire Square in danger by coming here," I said.

Audrey didn't say anything. I glanced over at her as we crossed a street and saw she was deep in thought. But when we stepped up onto the curb on the far side of the road and proceeded down the sidewalk on the shadier side of the street, she just shook her head.

"No, whoever else is out here that can touch your mind and maybe even cast spells through you, they're the one that put the Square in danger. You were never going to work any magic on Troy McFarland. Not to make him confess. Not even to stop him from grabbing me."

"I was totally prepared to knock him on his butt," I promised her. "But more like with a shove."

I demonstrated the motion with my hands as we walked, and Audrey responded with a brief laugh.

But one that was quickly gone. I could sense we were both thinking of the same thing in that moment.

Just who was it that had been there, watching us?

"Did you feel anything at all?" I asked.

She didn't need to ask me what I meant. She just sadly shook her head.

"Not a single thing," she said. Then she shot me a single anxious look. "Not that I was looking or anything. Maybe if I'd been on alert, I'd have felt something."

She was chewing her lip, and I could almost hear her inner monologue, berating herself for not being aware enough. Like she should've known to be on high alert.

I suspected that inner monologue was borrowing a lot of her old ritual magic academy teachers' voices.

And I further suspected that if those teachers had been anything like mine, lectures about how you weren't measuring up to standards could go on for quite some time.

I had to say something to derail that.

But what?

"Steph never felt anything in Geneva," I told her at last.

"Really?" she asked. She was tucking her hair behind her ears again, but the look in her eyes was bordering on hopeful.

"Not a thing. He just trusted my feelings and got us out of there in a hurry," I said. "That's why he knows whoever it was must have been a high level wizard."

"There really aren't that many of those," Audrey said. "Especially with the Wizard looking, there's only so long someone like that can keep hiding."

"I think you're right," I told her.

But as we drew within eyeshot of the Loose Leaves Teashop, I couldn't help worrying about what would happen first.

Would the Wizard figure out who was magically stalking me and put a stop to it?

Or would my magical stalker reveal themselves to me at a moment of their choosing?

I trusted the Wizard with all my heart and soul.

But the second option felt far too likely to me.

And I had no clue what this stranger wanted from me, and what that moment of revelation was going to mean.

CHAPTER

FOURTEEN

Audrey unlocked the teashop door to let us both inside, then promptly locked it again.

"Aren't you going to open for business?" I asked.

"No, I'm going upstairs to see Liam," she said. Then, very belatedly, she added, "Hopefully, he has another lead or two for us."

"Sure," I said. But she wasn't fooling me. After everything that had just happened, she wanted a moment alone with her boyfriend. And I could scarcely blame her.

I was pretty lucky that mine could show up anywhere in the world the minute I so much as thought of his name.

She was halfway to the door on the Square side of the shop when she turned back to look at me. "You'll come find me after you talk to the Wizard, right?" she said.

"Absolutely," I said. "Hopefully, it doesn't take too long. The Wizard has this way of seeming to know what I want to say before I say it, anyway. It makes conversations brief."

"Liam and I will be at Barnardo's place, then," she said.

I gave her a wave as I watched her go out the door.

Then I closed my eyes and pictured the library at the top of the

107

Tower again. Crackling fire, tables cluttered with research materials, the lingering odor of tuna fish sandwiches.

The latter grew stronger, like way stronger. I could smell the caraway in the bread, even.

I opened my eyes to see the Wizard regarding me standing there on his hearthrug with my eyes closed. He had a triangle of sandwich in one hand with one of the corners bitten off and was chewing as he watched me.

"Sorry," I said. "Am I interrupting?"

"No, I was just waiting for you," he said. "Are you hungry?"

"No, I'm fine," I said. Then it took a deep breath. "I have to tell you something."

"Yes, I rather thought you might," he said. Then he waved me to the wing-backed chair opposite of his before settling into his own spot. He took another bite of sandwich, then gestured for me to speak.

"That feeling I had in Geneva, like someone was pressing on my mind? I had that again about an hour ago. Only here, in town," I said.

He chewed his sandwich thoughtfully, although the look on his face was more one of someone savoring a flavor, perhaps as part of a taste test, than someone thinking about the words I had just spoken.

He took another bite, and I felt compelled to go on. Only when I tried, all my words came out in a nervous stammer. "There was a man, a prosaic. He was a little pushy... I mean, I don't think he was actually going to hurt Audrey. But he was definitely making her uncomfortable. And when he tried to grab her, I just wanted him to... stop. So I did. Make him stop, I mean."

I realized I was twisting my hands together in my lap over and over again. I forced them to stop, to stretch out flat over my thighs and remain still.

It took a lot of effort. It was like I had ants under my skin.

The Wizard finished the last bite of his sandwich and reached for a copper mug that was sitting on the table beside his chair. I heard the fizz of carbonation as he sipped at whatever was inside. And the bubbles popping filled the air with the smell of ginger and lime juice.

Then he set the mug aside again to look at me sharply.

"This was not your usual magic, then," he said. And he gestured at the sliver bracelet on my wrist, as if reminding me it was still there.

"No, there was no communication between me and the charm," I said. "The magic just flowed."

"Through you, but not of you?" he asked. His voice was still so sharp. It really did feel like I was in the principal's office answering for my latest mishap.

"Steph thinks—" I started to say, but he interrupted me by simply raising one wizened hand. My words stopped so abruptly I bit down on my own lip and tasted a drop of blood on my tongue.

"I will get Steph's assessment in due time," he said. But the sharpness was gone now. His tone was the kindly one I was more accustomed to. "I want to know what *you* think. No, I want to know what you felt. When it happened. Leave the theories to me."

"All right," I said. I spread my hands over my thighs again as I closed my eyes and called the memory back to the front of my mind.

"It was like a tidal wave," I said, my eyes still closed. "It was like power drew away from me, then came crashing back only ten times as strong. Only all that was in an instant. Out, then in, then whoosh. Then Troy was on the ground."

"And the bracelet never spoke to you?" the Wizard asked.

"No," I said, my eyes still closed, my mind still reliving that moment. "I think... Sorry. You didn't want me to do that."

"No, finish your thought," he said.

"I think it didn't speak to me because there was no time," I said. Then, even with my eyes still closed, I shook my head. "No, that's not it. It didn't speak to me because I wasn't intending to do anything. At least, not anything magical. I reached out to Troy, but I was only going to grab his arm, to stop him from grabbing Audrey. I was never going to use magic on him at all."

"No, of course not," the Wizard said, as if he had zero doubts that was true. "You were out in the prosaic world. The training you've had since you started at your very first academy has locked down your instincts, all our instincts, very strongly in that regard. It takes a strong will to use magic outside of our safe places. And it nearly never happens as a spontaneous, unintentional act."

"But in the alley when I fought Taurus Vernon—"

"The alley is a gray area, as close to the base of this Tower as it is," the Wizard said.

"Then what happened?" I asked, finally opening my eyes to look at him. Reliving that moment was providing no more new insights. And the feeling that I had in that moment been used as someone else's tool was getting uncomfortably strong.

"You've studied tidal waves?" he asked mildly. He wasn't even looking at me. His attention had gone back to the copper mug on his end table as he reached for it to take another sip of whatever ginger concoction lurked inside.

"Not specifically," I said.

"No, with your wide-ranging reading appetite, I'm sure you've just gathered the basics," he said.

"I guess?" I said.

He put the mug back, then folded his hands on his lap. "You know the basic mechanics of the event, is what I mean. Sometimes the trough of the wave reaches the shore before the peak. That leads to a drawback of water from the shore before the peak crashes."

"I guess?" I said again.

He smiled at me indulgently. "Your brain draws metaphors from what it knows. In your case, a large part of that is what you've read. You've experienced something that might be ineffable in the moment, but your brain finds the closest corollary and that defines the memory for you."

"Does this have anything to do with what Steph was telling me about modifying memories?" I asked, rubbing at my head. I wasn't getting a headache, exactly. It was more like I felt like I should be getting a headache. I hadn't tried to think so hard since I'd left school.

"Not exactly," he said with another fond smile. "I only meant it's interesting how you described this. Not as a tidal wave that overwhelmed you, but as a tsunami that pulled back, then slammed through you. Is that correct?"

I closed my eyes again. Was it correct? I had described it that way to the Wizard, but I hadn't been thinking about the words that closely when I'd spoken them.

So now I was revisiting the memory again.

And the answer was there.

"Yes," I said with absolute confidence. "Power was pulled from me first. Not enough, not as much as washed through me to pound Troy. But something was taken from me first."

"Interesting," the Wizard said, steepling his fingers together.

"But what does it mean?" I asked.

He looked up at me in surprise. "Mean? I have no idea. But it's definitely interesting, isn't it?"

I just gaped at him. Then I realized I was doing it and made a conscious effort to close my mouth.

"You should perhaps stick closer to the Square until we have this figured out," he said.

"But the investigation," I said.

"Yes, well," he said, tapping his steepled fingers against his chin. "Honestly, I find it very unlikely the culprit is in the prosaic world. But if they are, Steph should be the one to handle that part of the investigation."

"He has so much on his plate already, though," I said. Then I heard how accusatory my words came out and felt my cheeks heating to what had to be a bright shade of red.

"Are you going to take me to task for overworking my apprentice?" he asked me.

Now he was a master of tone. *His* words were pitched just so, so that I couldn't tell if he was joking with me, or warning me to stick to my lane.

And his intense gaze was holding me in place, not letting me go until I gave my answer.

"No," I said, just resisting the urge to add, *sir*.

"Good," he said. Then he planted his hands on the arms of his chair to leverage himself back up to his feet. "As I said, I'm sure the answer lies in magical grounds. No need to bother my overworked apprentice at all for that. But in the meantime, perhaps you'd like to check in with your companion before you return to your investigation?"

It took me a moment to work out that he was talking about Houdini.

"Yes, of course," I said. "How is Miss Snooty Cat doing?"

The Wizard didn't answer, but the sudden sadness in his eyes spoke more than any words.

He gestured for me to follow, and I did so.

I really hoped that matagot was going to pull through. I hoped it so much, there was nothing left in me to even feel the irony of that emotion.

I just really hoped Miss Snooty Cat was going to be okay.

FIFTEEN

Miss Snooty Cat had been moved to one of the spare bedrooms in the middle section halfway up the Tower. Another out-of-season fire was crackling in the fireplace there, bathing the windowless, stone-walled room in warm light. The bed was narrow, but more than large enough for the matagot's form.

It looked like she had shrunk. Even since I had seen her last, she looked smaller.

Houdini was curled up on the seat of a leather club chair that had been pulled close to the bedside. Curled up tight, but not napping. His large brown eyes were open as the Wizard and I came into the room, and he sat up at once when he saw me.

"How is she?" I asked him as I put a hand on his head, stroking around his incongruously droopy ears.

"Not better," he said. "No, I think she is getting worse."

"Worse?" I said, looking with alarm to the Wizard.

"Houdini is right," he said as he examined Miss Snooty Cat's paws and stroked her ears.

"And Barnardo? Have you heard?" I asked, almost choking on the question.

"Barnardo is still in a coma, but his vital signs are strong," the Wizard assured me. "He seems to be improving, even as Miss Snooty Cat is worsening."

"Is there a connection?" I asked.

"Perhaps," the Wizard said. "But more likely it's a matter of body size and dosage."

"The poison was in the cream," Houdini said. "Miss Snooty Cat drank a dishful, while Barnardo only had a sip. And he is so much larger than she is."

"That does seem to be the gist of it," the Wizard said. "But we still have no idea what poison was used."

"I'm working on it," I promised. "In fact, I should probably get back to Barnardo's apartment to see if Liam and Audrey have any more leads."

Houdini made a little squeaking sound, and I looked down at him in surprise. "Are you okay?"

"Yes," he said, ducking his head. "I just... well, I miss you. But I know you have to go. And I have to remain here," he added, lifting his chin as he spoke those words in my mind with the noblest of airs.

"Can I get you anything?" I asked. "Do you need any of your food or anything?"

"No, the Wizard fetched my food already," he said. "He even brought me that book, although I admit I don't have the heart to peruse it."

I looked in the direction he had nodded his head and saw the book Liam had taken, the one about dragons. It was resting on a chest of drawers opposite the foot of the bed.

"It's a very interesting text," the Wizard said. "I've already made copies for my library, as well as for your own use. It will take some time to read through it all, time which we sadly don't have at the moment. But that's the original there, if you need to return it to its owner."

"Thanks, I probably should," I said, picking it up. I looked at Houdini, and he gave me a little nod of permission.

"We have a copy in the nook inside the bookshop," he said. "Dragons live for centuries, you know. We have plenty of time to unlock the mystery of which kind I am."

"Of course," I said.

But his words triggered a sudden thought, one I didn't like at all.

Dragons lived for centuries, that was true. But rat terrier chihuahuas did not.

And I still didn't know if his appearance was only an illusion—albeit a very thorough illusion—or was the result of an actual transformation.

If the latter, we really didn't have unlimited time.

A decade, two at the most.

But surely we'd have answers before then.

I mustered up a smile for him as I pressed the book close to my chest. "I'll see you soon, Houdini. Dinnertime for sure, okay?"

"I'll be here, with Miss Snooty Cat," he said, and resumed his tight curled up posture on the seat of the chair.

"Oh, and before I forget," I said to the Wizard, and dug the potion bottles out of my pockets. "I found these in the house of a man who was buying things from Barnardo."

"Oh, my," the Wizard said, taking the bottles from me one by one and examining their labels. "Love and confidence."

"I know," I said, wincing. "I know it's against the law. But is it as bad if they don't have any magic in them as if they really do?"

"Neither is good," the Wizard said, holding one of the bottles towards the light from the fireplace and peering through it. "But we should find out which is the case before telling the authorities."

"And we *have* to tell them?" I asked.

He just gave me a very level look that made me squirm harder than if he'd actually delivered me the lecture on ethics I probably deserved.

"Right," I said. Now I had to be sure to save Barnardo's life, so he could forgive me for digging up dirt in his. And it was time to get back to work.

"Tabitha?" the Wizard said before I had quite closed my eyes to start picturing Barnardo's bedroom.

"Yes?"

"That feeling you had, of someone pressing on your mind?" he said. Mildly, as if we were merely discussing a television program we'd both seen.

"Yes?" I said again.

"If you feel it again, do be sure to come back here at once," he said. "You are able to move here much more quickly than you seem to imagine. Just wish it, and you'll be inside my library. No need to worry in an emergency that you don't have enough time to trigger the teleportation."

"Right," I said. I wondered just how long he had been studying me while I stood there on his hearthrug with my eyes closed, imagining all the aspects of the library I was already standing inside.

I must've looked like a real dope.

"It's instantaneous. And I assure you, you cannot be followed," he said.

He was still speaking mildly, and I suddenly realized this was for Houdini's benefit. He didn't want Houdini to worry about me.

And he would. If he knew what had happened with Troy, he would be very worried indeed.

Poor little guy. Worrying about Miss Snooty Cat was all he could handle at the moment. Clearly, or he would still be studying that dragon book while he waited for her to stir.

"Dinnertime," I said to Houdini.

"Yes," he said, but his eyes were on Miss Snooty Cat.

I hugged the book again, then closed my eyes and imagined Barnardo's bedroom.

Which was easier said than done. I hadn't been paying that close of attention to those sorts of details when I had been there before. Did that bank of computers even *have* a smell?

Perhaps I should just aim for his kitchen.

Then I felt a tap, the Wizard's fingertips on my shoulder. I opened my eyes to look at him and saw a confusing blur of motion as the world around me spun in a kaleidoscope of images that were partly the spare bedroom in the Tower and partly Barnardo's room.

Then I blinked, and the world stopped moving. I was safely inside Barnardo's room.

I guess getting out of the Tower was not as instinctively easy as getting in was. But that made sense. I was working against its powerful pull. And my magic wasn't quite up to *that* challenge.

I saw Audrey leaning over the back of the office chair that held Liam hunched over the keyboard tray. She had her arms draped around his shoulders, high enough not to interfere with his typing, and the long wings of her hair were spread around him like a protective veil.

They weren't doing anything in particular, but it somehow still felt like an intimate moment. One I didn't want to interrupt. And yet I had just popped soundlessly into the middle of it.

I took half a step back, hoping to retreat at least into the hallway to make a second entrance with more of a warning to my approach. My sneakers made no sound on that thick carpeting.

But something still gave me away, because Audrey suddenly turned to look back at me. Her hair swung into Liam's face and he made a sound of protest as it momentarily blinded him.

"Sorry!" I said. I wanted to raise my hands in surrender, but I was still holding that heavy book.

"No worries. We were waiting for you," Audrey said, then pulled her hair back as she straightened up. "How is Barnardo? And Miss Snooty Cat?"

"Barnardo is a little better, Miss Snooty Cat is a little worse," I said. "But they're both hanging on. Any more leads?"

"So far, just one. But it's a good one," Audrey said. Then I heard the sound of the printer roaring back to life.

"Barnardo had a competitor," Liam said as he spun the chair around to face me. "A *local* competitor."

"And she's a witch," Audrey said.

"That's good," I said, thinking of the Wizard's admonishment to stick to magical areas.

But Audrey had no idea about any of that. She just raised a questioning eyebrow at me.

"Sorry, I didn't mean *good*," I said. "The lead is good. And given the likely nature of the poison used, the fact that it's actually a witch makes me think we're getting closer."

"Yeah, me, too," Liam said as he got up to fetch the pages from the now quiet printer.

"Is she downtown, then?" I asked. As densely populated as the Square was, it was still a single block of buildings. Most of the witches in Minneapolis lived in the multiple interconnected pockets that were hidden throughout the downtown area on the other side of the river.

But Audrey was shaking her head. "No, she's an outlier. She has a pocket of her own, hidden away in one of the suburbs."

"Not magical ground?" I asked nervously.

"Her house is," Audrey said. "It's been around as long as the Square, at least if prosaic property records are to be believed. But it's not an entire neighborhood. Just a single house."

"It's called the Crofts' Cottage," Liam said as he handed the pages to me. "'Cottage' makes it sound small, but given the neighborhood it's hiding in, I wouldn't be surprised if it turned out to be a modestly named mansion." He shrugged, as if that were something he saw every day.

Then he saw the book I was still hugging close to my chest.

"Are you done with that?" he asked anxiously. "I have to head to work soon, and it would be great if I could put that back before it's missed."

"Yes, the Wizard made copies," I said, holding the book out for him. He gave it a quick once-over as if checking it for signs of damage before stuffing into his backpack. "Thanks for letting us see it."

"Yeah, it's quite a coincidence, me finding that," he said as he closed the straps on his backpack.

"Coincidence," I said, rolling the word around in my mind.

That word kept popping up. And kept feeling like it wasn't quite appropriate.

I couldn't help remembering that he had only found his job in the first place because of a spell I had crafted for him.

The spell was a reworked version of a spell that helped a witch find answers to her questions. And I hadn't even been the one to cast it. That had been Audrey.

But I couldn't shake the feeling that somehow that spell which had been intended to help Liam find his perfect job had—also? or instead?—found the book that was just what Houdini and I had been looking for.

"Shall we?" Audrey asked, indicating the papers in my hands.

I looked down at the address on the top page. I didn't recognize the street name, and I was nowhere near familiar enough with zip codes to know which numbers were in which parts of town.

Liam must've read my thoughts on my face because, as he hoisted his backpack up onto his shoulder, he said, "it's in Prospect Park. That's in Minneapolis, but further east than here. But you can totally get a bus there."

"A bus," I said, and I knew I was visibly flinching.

"Tabitha?" Audrey asked with concern in her voice.

"It's just, the Wizard thinks I should avoid the prosaic world. For a while," I said.

"Oh, right," Audrey said. "Because of what happened before. Sure."

Liam looked back and forth between us, clearly not having a clue what we were talking about.

"Let's go down to the pub," Audrey said brightly. "Thaisa Wolsey knows all the routes the boats take through the tunnels. She can get us close to there, if not all the way there."

Then Liam laughed out loud. Audrey and I both looked at him in frank confusion.

"Sorry," he said, putting a hand over his mouth. "It's just, it would be pretty ironic if that location wasn't part of your magical network."

I exchanged a glance with Audrey, but she just shrugged, as clueless as I.

"Why is that?" I asked him.

"The water tower they have there is kind of famous," he said. When the confusion still didn't leave my or Audrey's faces, he pulled out his phone and tapped at the screen as he spoke. "It's more than a hundred years old, not a functioning water tower anymore. Colloquially, it's known as the Witch's Hat. Granted, that's just because of its shape. I've never heard any urban legends about actual witches being connected to it."

Then he turned his phone screen towards us to show us a structure that did, indeed, look like a stereotypical witch's hat.

"You know we don't actually wear those," I said.

"Except ironically," Audrey said.

"Except ironically," I agreed.

"Oh, sure," he said as he tucked his phone away. "And for the record, I'm also aware that urban legends I may or may not have heard about witches have not tracked at all with the actual goings-on of Minnesota witches. Still, I bet you can find a magical route to that place, no problem."

"And I'll fill you in with what we know about this woman on the way," Audrey promised.

We walked Liam back to the door he was most familiar with, the one in the Loose Leaves Teashop. Then we headed to the Wolseys' Pub to start our journey across town.

CHAPTER
SIXTEEN

The Wolseys' Pub was the only restaurant in the Square. Although the blocks around us in the prosaic world were packed with a variety of cuisines, when I didn't feel like cooking dinner, I usually found myself crossing through the orchard to grab something warm and filling in the pub.

The interior was cozy, reminiscent of actual pubs I'd been to in England and Ireland. Everything from the wattle and daub walls to the heavy oak tables and chairs felt like it had been there for centuries. The wood planks of the floor had been worn into smooth grooves by countless boots and shoes. Even the food smells of roasted meat and potatoes as well as the ever present aroma of ale felt like they'd always been there, freshened daily but never diminishing.

The mullioned windows were few, small, and of a mottled sort of glass, letting in only a little of the light from outside. This was scarcely noticeable in the evenings, when the fire in the fireplace filled the spacious, high-ceilinged dining room with warmth and the candles burning on every table added enough light to see your dining companions.

But it was still too early for dinner, and with no customers sitting within, it made the space feel both larger and darker.

When Audrey and I stepped inside, we hovered near the doorway for a moment, waiting for our eyes to adjust. Almost as if she sensed the moment we could see well enough to recognize her, Thaisa Wolsey emerged from the kitchen. Her long, red hair was pulled back in a thick but short braid at the nape of her neck, and her clothes were a mashup of magical and prosaic fashions: a long emerald green tunic that looked Celtic but with its impractically large sleeves tied back with a cord in a Japanese style, and a worn and faded pair of designer blue jeans.

"Early dinner?" she asked as she wiped her just-washed hands dry on her apron. She was the same age as Audrey and I were, but had opted out of the higher magical academies we had both attended. She had instead done a few courses at a local school that focused on just the aspects of magic she needed to know to take over for her parents and run the pub after they retired.

It was very rare to run into her anywhere outside of the pub, and rarer still to find her anywhere when she wasn't trying to accomplish a thousand tasks at once.

"No, no dinner. We're heading downstairs to catch a boat," I said.

"Heading to the hospital?" she asked. "I know he's still in a coma, but even so, let Barnardo know we're all thinking about him, okay?"

"Actually, we're looking for someone else. In Prospect Park," I said.

"We're hoping she can help us figure out what happened to Barnardo," Audrey added.

"Prospect Park," Thaisa said with a ponderous frown.

"Her name is Ursula Croft?" Audrey said. "She lives in a place called Crofts' Cottage."

"Have you heard of her?" I asked.

Because unlike me, who had spent her entire life moving from place to place all over the world up until just a few months before, and unlike Audrey, who was from Mankato in the southern part of

Minnesota, Thaisa had lived in the Square in Minneapolis for her entire life.

But after a moment's thought, she shook her head. "No. Sorry. The name Croft sounds a little familiar? But also a little common."

"I get the sense she's a bit of a recluse anyway," Audrey said.

I looked at the thick stack of papers I was still clutching in my hands. I had only glanced at the top sheet so far, but it was clear that Liam had assembled quite a story in whatever he had printed out for me. Audrey knew at least some of it, I was sure. But I had no real idea where we were going.

I just had such a strong urge to keep moving, to keep working. Like that would help Barnardo somehow.

"The boats can take you to Prospect Park," Thaisa said. "You'll go up to the St. Anthony Falls, but stay with the river rather than crossing it into downtown. Then you'll catch the remnants of the Bridal Veil Creek that the prosaics buried years ago. There's still a falls there, but our ways are deeper, of course."

"And that takes us to this address?" I asked, squinting at the street name printed on the top sheet of the papers in my hands.

"Close enough," Thaisa said with a shrug. "There really isn't a community of us there, so there's no actual station. But the boat will wait for you."

I nodded. But I knew what she wasn't saying out loud.

Our ride would be waiting for us in the sewer. Granted, one of the deeper sewers where the buried creek still ran. But we'd have to climb out through more conventional sewers to get to the surface. And then just start walking around.

Well, I had made worse trips in my time.

"Thanks for your help," I said.

"I hope you find what you're looking for," Thaisa said. "Barnardo used to come in here every midafternoon to share a plate of fried potatoes with me on my break. And to gossip, of course. I hadn't realized how much that little break in the day meant to me. I don't get out much, but talking to Barnardo, it was like he was bringing the whole Square in for me."

"Ironically, this investigation would be so much easier with his help," I said. "He knew everyone, or at least could find out who they were much faster than we can without him."

"We'll find her," Audrey said, raising her chin as if stepping up to a challenge.

With one last nod of thanks to Thaisa, we passed through the kitchen and down the cold stone steps to the quay that was our station in the witches' underground transportation system.

The magical neighborhoods in New York had secret subways. The ones in Paris had catacombs no prosaic had ever found. The ones in Hong Kong were connected above ground, crossing the tops of buildings in a parkour system that was not for the faint-hearted.

And Minneapolis had its system of buried creeks and rivers, spreading like a watery web all through it and into neighboring St. Paul.

But, like the magical subways in New York, you needed a card to get a ride. Luckily, Audrey and I had acquired our own some time ago. We touched them to the art déco turnstile that waited incongru-ously next to the mostly clean storm runoff water that drained past the Square towards the Mississippi River.

And a short wait later, a boat appeared. There was no driver, just two bench seats and a tall prow from which hung a magical lantern that glowed an eerie shade of green. Audrey and I climbed on board and settled in.

"Prospect Park, please," Audrey said. Although I had my suspi-cions that wasn't even necessary. The boats always seemed to know what was needed of them.

We slipped away from the quay and headed down the dark tunnel with its stone arches that seemed far too grand for such a place.

I glanced down at the papers stacked on my lap, but the glossiness of the printer paper was too reflective, the ink of the text too dim, for me to make out much in the unnatural greenish light.

"Tell me about Ursula Croft," I said to Audrey. "She lives in a place called Crofts' Cottage, but that's all I've caught so far."

"She's a recluse," Audrey said.

"Yeah, I caught that too," I said with a grin.

"Right," Audrey smiled back at me. "She owns a business that sells potions to prosaics, called Croft's Concoctions. Judging from the look and limited functionality of her website, she's been around for a long time. Probably longer than Barnardo. But unlike the cottage, I don't think the business is a family thing. Because of the placements of the apostrophe. You know, Croft's singular, not Crofts' plural."

"Do Ursula and Barnardo know each other?" I asked.

"That's just the thing, we're not sure," Audrey said. "They have no direct communication with each other. If you could read what Liam printed out for you, it's mostly screen caps from various forums and social media places. Both Barnardo and Ursula Croft were using fake names. Multiple fake names."

"But they were interacting with each other pseudonymously?" I asked.

"Yeah, a lot," Audrey said. "Although Liam was pretty sure they weren't aware of how often they were talking to each other. Sometimes Barnardo would be friendly with one of Ursula's identities, but antagonistic to another, and vice versa. It's actually a bit of a mess. Who would go through all this work to pretend to be a bunch of people? And why?"

"Loneliness, I guess," I said.

"Barnardo had breakfast with the three of us every day," Audrey said. "Then he'd go see Titus Bloom for a coffee before going up to his apartment. Now we know he also stopped into the pub every afternoon to chat with Thaisa. Given how much he knows about everyone in the Square, he's clearly talking to other people, maybe even on the same kind of schedule. We just haven't discovered it yet. And he always had Miss Snooty Cat."

"I know," I said. "That still doesn't mean he didn't feel lonely, though. Maybe he was looking for some kind of connection we just weren't giving him."

Audrey chewed her lip for a minute. "He never said anything."

"No, he didn't," I agreed.

But he had always felt... well, like he was lonely. I knew the feeling well, having spent my life surrounded by other students who talked to me because they had to, but never really connected with me.

"We should've noticed anyway," Audrey said.

"We don't know what he was or is feeling," I said. "But we can ask him when he wakes up."

Audrey nodded, but resumed chewing her lip.

We had reached the river, but just as Thaisa had said, rather than taking the channel that dove down below the magically recreated remnants of the once mighty St. Anthony Falls, we instead turned to follow the river as it began its meander towards St. Paul.

"This Ursula Croft, is she breaking the rules of our community too?" I asked.

"Maybe?" Audrey said. "Judging from the comments left on her product pages, she has satisfied customers. Or had. Nothing had been updated in years. Or rather, decades. It was very old web design. You couldn't even order online. It was technically a mail-order catalog that you could browse in a very limited way on her website. But you still had to write in to place an order."

"Weird," I said. "If she was on all the forums and that, like Barnardo was, wouldn't that make her also extremely online?"

I knew the words sounded funny coming out of my mouth.

But Audrey just shrugged.

The boat beneath us bobbed a few times, like an athlete preparing to make their move. Then, as the aqueous ceiling of the channel above us shifted from a smooth bluish-green of steadily moving water to the fractals of expanding rings as we reached the bottom of the Bridal Veil Waterfall, the boat dipped and plunged through a deeper channel.

There was a confused moment where I wasn't sure *where* we were heading. The waterfall broke up the light from above, and the lantern hanging from the prow of our boat was swinging wildly.

Then we left the sunlight behind, sliding once more into a subterranean stone-walled tunnel. The green light from the lantern danced slickly over the damp walls, but barely lit the surface of great patches of what I really, really hoped was moss.

The air around us was damp and chill, but the only smell was a slight odor of rotting plant matter. Normal storm sewer smell. Not pleasant, unless you were comparing it to a septic sewer.

Then the boat lurched to a halt so suddenly that both Audrey and I were catching hold of the sides of the boat in near panic.

We had stopped at the base of a ladder, metal rungs set directly in the stone wall of the tunnel. The rungs went up and up, past the point where the green lantern light could reach.

"I guess this is our stop," I said, folding the papers to stuff them into one of the cargo pockets on my pants.

I was so glad that Violenta Court insisted on copious pockets in all of her designs. They were a real lifesaver.

I grabbed onto the rung of the ladder that was at my shoulder height, then put my feet on the bottom rung just above the reach of the oily-looking water.

And then I started to climb.

CHAPTER

SEVENTEEN

The grate at the top of the sewer was on hinges and opened easily at my touch. So, while we might not be in a magical neighborhood per se, it was definitely one that was visited by magical types often enough for someone to make the path convenient.

But it had been a long climb up the ladder, and I was happy to sit down on the curb and rest for a minute while I waited for Audrey to climb out behind me. My arms were trembling a little. But mostly, after touching rung after rung of damp yet gritty metal, I longed to wash my hands.

The sun was just starting to set, but the sticky heat was still going strong. We were at the end of an alley that snaked between the backs of street-facing properties, and where that alley met the road was dominated by two ancient oak trees. They had been planted on either side of the alley, but their branches tangled together over the top of it in a living archway.

Their roots were doing a number on the sidewalk, too. Perhaps not surprisingly, the families walking with strollers and the runners jogging by with earbuds in were all doing it on the far side of the road, where the sidewalk was smoother.

But I knew magical interference when I saw it. This alley had to lead to Ursula Croft's house. But the trees that were subtly directing prosaics away from noticing the narrow alley were far too old to be her work.

"Crofts' Cottage," I said to Audrey as she flopped down to rest beside me. "Sounds like a family place, right? Like it's been here a while?"

She was rubbing the palms of her hands on her pants but looked up at the trees, then at the neighborhood around us.

"Liam said the water tower was built in 1913," Audrey said. We both looked around, but if we were within eyeshot of the Witch's Hat Tower, there were too many trees between for us to make it out. "I suppose some of the houses could be older. Still, not as old as the Square though. Do you think?"

"The Square isn't the oldest magical neighborhood in the Twin Cities," I said. "That would be the underground city in the caves under St. Paul."

"I'll take my lovely, sunny apartment in the Square over living in a subterranean city, thanks," Audrey said, wrinkling her nose at the thought.

"Shall we go see what this place looks like?" I asked, getting to my feet.

"Sure," Audrey sighed. But she took my hand when I offered it to her and scrambled to her feet as well.

The further we walked along that narrow alleyway, the quieter the world around us became. I looked back to see the branches of the trees behind us even more tightly knit together than before. So it had opened up for us?

Then I heard Audrey's breath catch and switched from looking back over my shoulder to looking at the cottage coming into view before us.

It had cute cottage features like a thatched roof of golden straw, with sprouts of green poking out here and there, and round windows of sparkling beveled glass, and great swathes of ivy growing everywhere.

But it was also, frankly, huge. And the closer we got, the larger it loomed over us.

I had seen smaller government buildings.

The alley ended at a gate in a white privacy fence. But when I reached out to knock on that gate, it swung away from my hand, almost inviting us in.

"I guess we're expected?" I said.

Audrey just shrugged.

Beyond the gate, the path underfoot switched from dirt road to brick walkway. The bricks were spaced apart, and sprigs of thyme as thick as moss grew between them. Their herby scent filled the air with each step we took. More herbs grew in thick clumps all around us. I recognized lavender and rosemary, mugwort and sage, chamomile and lemon balm, and dozens more plants I'd need a closer look at to identify.

But they were all growing in lush abundance, despite their varied growing seasons, and despite the fact that many weren't really meant to grow in Minnesota's particular climate.

"She definitely has magic of some variety, whether she's using it in her potions or not," I said to Audrey. I was whispering even though we seemed to be alone. But when trees moved and gates opened up at your arrival, it was probably safer to assume you could also be heard.

"It's the cottage," a voice said, and we both jumped. Then I saw the speaker, standing in the shadows at the corner of the house as if she'd just come around from the back. She was dressed for gardening with a wide-brimmed hat, an apron with pockets designed to hold a variety of tools, and a pair of dirt-stained gloves she was just tugging off one finger at a time.

"We didn't mean to intrude," I said.

"You couldn't even if you had meant to," she said, not quite interrupting me, but close to it.

"Ursula Croft?" Audrey said.

"Yes," she said. Gloves off, she tucked them into a pocket of that apron then stepped forward, into the dying light from the sun. "You have the advantage of me."

"I'm Tabitha Greene," I said. "And this is Audrey Mirken. We were hoping to talk to you, if you could spare a moment?"

"Talk to me about what?" she asked.

I glanced at Audrey before answering, "About your business?"

It seemed like a safer way into the conversation than mentioning Barnardo's name, or his business's name.

"Croft's Concoctions?" she asked doubtfully.

"Yes, that's the one," I said. Did she have others?

"But surely the two of you don't need anything like that," she said. Her watery blue eyes swept over me and then Audrey in silent assessment. "You're both witches, or the cottage would not have let you in."

I felt a bizarre rush of pleasure at those words. Like I needed the validation from a magical cottage.

Still, it was nice to have. I had spent too many years being told I wasn't a proper witch, I guess.

"It's a little complicated," Audrey said.

"Have you heard of MacBeth's Marvels?" I asked.

If she had any intention of denying it, the instant look of revulsion that crossed her face at the mention of the name made that completely impossible.

And she seemed to recognize that fact.

"That company is my chief competitor. But I'm not sure how any of this is any concern of yours," she said.

"MacBeth's Marvels has only been around for a couple of years," I said. "How big was its impact on your sales?"

"Almost negligible," she said with a sniff. "My branding is first rate. My customers are very loyal. He exploited a few markets I wasn't even actively pursuing. I suppose he's had a modicum of success with it, but frankly they were markets I wasn't pursuing for a reason. He can have them."

"What markets?" Audrey asked.

But I was distracted by another thought. Ursula kept saying "he." Did that mean she already knew Barnardo was the person running MacBeth's Marvels? Or was she just speaking generally, and a bit old-fashionedly?

"I stick with beauty items myself," Ursula said to Audrey. "I don't make any promises about certain outcomes. Not like he does."

"I haven't seen your website," I said. "But I have seen MacBeth's Marvels. Can you be more specific? Do you mean you're not promising magic to your customers?"

"There are rules about such things," she said haughtily.

"There are," I agreed. Then I looked at Audrey.

Audrey had seen the website. And judging from the little wince she directed my way, Ursula Croft was not being entirely honest with us. I tipped my head towards Ursula, all but begging Audrey to say what she was thinking.

Audrey tucked her hair behind her ears, then cleared her throat softly before speaking. "You don't put extravagant claims on your website, that is true. But most of your sales don't come through your website."

"How on Earth do you know that?" Ursula asked.

But Audrey ignored the question. "In fact, none of your purchases are processed through your website. They are all handled through email. And those emails are from longstanding customers. All of your new customers are referrals."

"I rather think that speaks to the quality of my business," Ursula said. But her eyes were still narrowed in suspicion.

The intensity in those now icy eyes was making Audrey nervous. She shifted her weight from foot to foot. But she pressed on. "The thing is, in those emails, you make a lot of strong claims. In fact, you make exactly the sorts of claims that are against the rules you just mentioned."

"Prove it," Ursula said, practically spitting the words out into Audrey's face.

But I just pulled the papers out of my cargo pocket and showed them to her. She couldn't see what was printed on them since they were still folded in half, but she could see the size of the stack.

"These are just printouts of your communications," I told her. "Our friend has access to all the emails."

"How?" Ursula asked, now frankly flabbergasted.

"Your website is old. And your security is really not very good," Audrey said. She sounded almost apologetic.

Then, for whatever reason, all the growing anger just drained out of Ursula before our eyes. Her shoulders dropped, and she passed a hand over her face. When she looked up at the two of us again, she was much calmer.

"Why don't we step inside," she said resignedly. "I fear you were right when you said it before. This is going to get complicated."

CHAPTER

EIGHTEEN

Ursula pushed open the cottage door and led us into the sort of spacious entryway framed by two massive staircases that cottages tended not to have. She hung her hat and apron from one of a row of hooks near the door, then gestured for us to follow her past the staircases towards the back of the house.

As imposing as that entryway had been, the kitchen we found beyond it was more cottage-appropriate. There was a fireplace set in one wall, currently unlit but featuring a variety of cauldrons and kettles hanging from metal hooks that could swing back over the flames or out over the hearth. Two ovens were built into the brick on either side of the fireplace, and to judge by the shiny spots on their door handles, they saw a lot of use.

The walls featured heavy timbers that supported rafters above. And beyond that, I could see the thatch roof itself. But between us and the roof were row after row of hanging herbs in various stages of drying.

"Do all these herbs go into your concoctions?" I asked.

"These? No, they're a little too potent for that," Ursula said airily as she crossed the room to open the door of the heavy, old-fashioned icebox. "Iced tea?"

"That would be lovely," I said.

"This is a very unusual house for this neighborhood," Audrey said conversationally as she peeked out the window over the sink and into the back garden beyond.

My attention was caught by the sink itself. It was as much an antique as that icebox, with separate faucets for hot and cold water. If you wanted something in between, you'd have to use the rubber plug to stop up the bottom and fill the basin from both faucets.

That sounded like a real pain.

Not surprisingly, there was no sign of a dishwasher. Or even a stove besides that functional fireplace.

"We Crofts have been here longer," Ursula said as she banged three glasses down on the kitchen table that was as thick as a butcher's block. Then she filled them each about halfway from a pickling jar full of tea so dark I could taste the bitterness on my tongue just looking at it.

"Really?" Audrey said. "So the neighborhood grew up around you?"

"Like parasites," Ursula said. "Invasive species. We couldn't keep them away."

"You kept a pocket to yourself, anyway," I said. "Those trees are very strong magic."

"Yes," she said, but something darkened her eyes. A sad memory, perhaps. "My great-grandmother planted those. Her grandfather was the one who built this house. His magic infuses the foundation, and his daughter and son-in-law wove the spells that maintain the gardens and the gate. The trees at the end of the alley were her contribution. And with those, Crofts' Cottage was complete."

I guessed that Ursula was a little older than Barnardo, perhaps late thirties. Counting back to her great-grandmother's time... that might just explain the age of the icebox and sink.

"Nothing new since then?" Audrey asked.

"Don't need it," Ursula grunted, then swallowed down half of her iced tea in one long swig.

I took a sip of mine and found it just as bitter as I had feared. I set it down far enough away from my hands that I wouldn't be tempted to pick it up again.

Audrey never touched hers at all.

"Nothing at all?" Audrey asked. She was still using her conversational tone, but I sensed she was driving towards something. I said nothing, waiting to hear Ursula's response.

The look of revulsion that had crossed Ursula's face at the mention of MacBeth's Marvels was nothing compared to the one on her face now. "Nothing added to the cottage? Why does that question sound so judgmental? What, do you think I need anything the subhuman world provides? Like electricity, perhaps? Or perhaps you're thinking of a *phone line*."

She uttered those last words with dripping disdain, then turned her attention back to her iced tea, not noticing the horrified look that Audrey and I were sharing.

Calling nonmagical people prosaics was something I was just barely comfortable with. It still felt a little condescending, but other words were so much worse.

Words like "normal" or "mundane," I mean.

Words like "subhuman?"

I shuddered. Somehow, the bitterness that lingered on my tongue after my sole sip of Ursula's tea felt all too appropriate.

"But your company sells products to the prosaics," Audrey said. And she managed to get all those words out without any sarcasm or irony. Something I'm sure I would've failed at if I had tried.

I mean, we already knew she was partaking of the technology she was happily sneering at. She was, as Audrey had said, extremely online.

But all Ursula said was, "Meh." Which didn't tell us anything at all.

"It *is* your company, right?" I said.

"I can't live on herbs alone," she said.

I shot a look of puzzlement at Audrey. But Audrey just looked thoughtful.

"I see," she said. "Your ancestors' magic keeps your cottage running. And the garden. You have an infinite supply of herbs."

"For what that's worth," Ursula said, looking down into her glass of iced tea as if she had spotted a bug floating in there.

"But you have no family money or anything like that," Audrey said.

"Not as such," Ursula grumbled. "The cottage is worth some-thing, but only if I sell it. And I can't do that. It's been in the family for generations. I'm stuck here. My only option was to sell those concoctions to the subhumans."

I wanted to call her out for using that word again, but Audrey caught my eye and gave me a quick shake of the head.

We were here to investigate, for Barnardo's sake. My personal feelings had to be put aside.

For the moment, anyway.

"I don't understand, though," Audrey said, still in her breezy voice. "The cottage grows all these herbs for you, very potent herbs, but those *aren't* the ones you're selling?"

"No. I told you. There's no need," Ursula said. "My customers believe every single thing I tell them. And they tell their friends, and they believe it too."

"But there's no actual magic in any of it?" I asked.

"What use do those people have for real magic? They chose to step away from it centuries ago," she said.

I bit down hard on my lip. That was definitely one theory. But it wasn't anything like the consensus view. Given the current structure of the world, it was far more likely we magical types had chosen to step away from the prosaics.

But this wasn't the time for that argument.

"I know you think my little emails mean I was breaking the rules of our community, but I wasn't," she said. She poured herself another glass of that bitter tea and swallowed a measure of it, smacking her lips as if she relished the flavor. Which, frankly, she must. I could see the leaves of a stevia plant growing on the windowsill over her sink, right there if she wanted it.

"I just need a little bit of income to keep myself and this place afloat," she went on. "I'll leave the actual rule-bending and rule-breaking to the likes of Barnardo Daley."

I pounced on that at once. "So you *do* know him!"

"I never said I didn't," she said with a gleam to her eye I didn't like at all.

"You certainly pretended otherwise," I said.

"I did not," she said.

"You don't particularly like Barnardo, do you?" Audrey asked.

"What's to like?" she said with a too-casual shrug. "I mean, does *anyone* like that man?"

"We do," I said. "That's why we're here."

"To defend his honor?" Ursula said with a sneer. "He sullied that himself, I assure you. Nothing I've said about him or his company is remotely libelous."

"We're not defending his honor," Audrey said. "Surely you've heard he's not well?"

"In trouble for selling magic to the subhumans?" she asked with another sneer.

"In a coma," I snapped at her. "In a coma he might not come out of. Not unless Audrey and I can figure out just what magical *concoction* he was poisoned with." She flinched at that word, half of the name of her business, but recovered almost instantly to meet my hard stare with haughty defiance.

"I'm sure that has nothing to do with me," she said.

"Can you prove it?" I asked. I lifted my hands toward the ceiling, where more herbs than I could name without referencing some sort of guidebook hung in drying bundles. Then I gestured towards the bay window over the sink, its sill filled with culinary and medicinal plants in pots.

Then beyond that, to the gardens themselves.

"Poison gardens are traditional in some families," Audrey said. "I suppose that must be what those plants are at your back fence. The ones that are growing in decorative cages. Very traditional."

"That's just for show," Ursula said. But her eyes were starting to dart around nervously. Like she was trying to make sure something she didn't want us to see was safely out of sight.

"To show whom?" I asked.

It was a stab in the dark. But Ursula struck me as someone who didn't exactly have an abundance of friends.

And I guess I hit the mark, as her face first blanched and then reddened to a furious, almost purple color.

"I didn't poison Barnardo Daley," she said. "I had no reason to. I've been very clear, his business was no threat to mine."

"Personal animosity is just as good a motive for some people," I said.

She was breathing hard, her hands fisting and unfisting over and over again. But in the end, she sounded remarkably calm as she said, "The burden of proof is yours."

"True enough," I said cheerily. "But perhaps you would like to aid us in clearing your name? All we need is a green bottle and permission to stroll through your cottage and gardens."

"By all means," she said. She opened a cupboard over the icebox and came out with a heavy bottle of green glass that had once contained wine of some sort, but was now quite clean. She set it on the butcher block tabletop and stepped back.

Audrey took a deep breath, then lifted her wand and began the incantation that was becoming old hat to her. I merely waited until the kitchen was filled with the kaleidoscope of green lights. Then I helped Audrey open every cupboard as well as the icebox and even the oven doors beside the fireplace.

We rustled through the herbs hanging overhead to be sure nothing was hiding higher up in the rafters that was glowing that telltale shade of green.

Ursula opened the backdoor for us, and we carried the bottle out into the garden. The sun was out of the sky now, the first stars only just emerging as the indigo darkened overhead. It would be easy to see anything that lit up as poisonous in that fading light.

But nothing did. Not even the plants that hung in the cages at the back of the yard.

When we came back inside the kitchen, we found Ursula standing with another door open for us. This led us down into the stone-walled cellar. It ran the entire length and width of the cottage, but it was still very difficult to move around down there. Only narrow corridors cut paths through the stacks and stacks of boxes filled with products bearing the Croft's Concoctions logo.

We opened a few, but nothing gave off any glow.

And then the last of the spell faded from the bottle, and Audrey and I were in darkness.

"What do you think?" Audrey asked me. We could both sense Ursula waiting for us at the top of those rickety wooden steps. But unless she was using magic, I doubted she could hear us.

"I think she is just what she says she is," I said. "She sells products she knows do nothing to people she doesn't think are worthy of real magic. And she lies to them about it with no remorse."

Then I heaved a long sigh before going on. "But I don't think she poisoned Barnardo."

"There were things out there that aren't strictly speaking safe for consumption," Audrey said. "But I agree. I don't see any sign of actual poison."

"Did you girls want to check my attic?" Ursula sing-songed down to us.

I ignored her, choosing instead to take out a bottle of shampoo from the nearest box. I squinted at the label, then opened the cap to sniff at the contents.

Rosemary and mint.

"She claims that will give you longer, thicker, more lustrous hair," Audrey said.

"Good luck achieving that without at least a little lavender or hibiscus," I said.

"Is this a dead end, then?" Audrey asked.

"For now, I think so," I said.

We climbed back up out of the cellar. I tried to ignore the smug look on Ursula's face as she shut the cellar door behind us.

"If you think of anything that might be helpful—" I started to say.

"What on Earth could I know that might be helpful?" she sneered.

"I'm asking myself the same thing," I said, finally letting some of my irritation show. "Do you have any skill at this sort of thing at all? The cottage is giving you scads and scads of excellent plants. And you aren't even using any to sweeten your tea, let alone improve the lives of others."

She looked like she had a response to that, but I pressed on before she could sputter it out.

"As I was saying, if you think of anything that might help us treat Barnardo's magical poisoning and bring him back out of his coma, please let us or the Wizard know," I said.

The flush of color drained out of her cheeks, and I sensed a sharp retort had just died on her tongue. She swallowed hard, twice, her skin deathly pale, before she could summon words again.

"The Wizard?" she repeated, almost in a whisper. "He's involved in this?"

"He's very involved," I said. Then I took the papers out of my pocket once more. I unfolded them, then smoothed them down flat on her kitchen counter. I put my finger down on top of the entire thick stack of printouts. "You've said a lot of things on these pages. I certainly hope you'll think about some of those things you said. Maybe think about what you could've said instead. But I guess I'm not holding my breath."

Then I turned away, heading back towards her front door, Audrey close behind me.

But Ursula chased after us, catching up just as we reached the doorway.

"You'll tell the Wizard I had nothing to do with this?" she asked, almost breathless.

I blinked at her. "I can't tell him that. I don't know that that's even true. But if you want to tell him yourself, I'd suggest having more to back it up with than your glow of innocence."

"It's a little tarnished," Audrey added.

Then we both left the cottage behind. Which was a pity. It was truly an enchanted place, doing the best it could. A shame it's only remaining ward was really a terrible human being.

But, alas, probably not a murderer.

We still had more work to do.

CHAPTER

NINETEEN

If a few months before, anyone would've told me that I'd spend an entire night sleeping curled up in a chair pulled close to the sickbed of a certain Miss Snooty Cat, I probably would've laughed out loud.

And if they'd told me that Houdini would be there with me, on my lap but decidedly not sleeping as he watched the matagot's slow, uneven breathing with anxious eyes, I would've had real doubts about their sanity.

And yet, there I was. Curled up in a club chair, Houdini on my lap with his nose resting on my shoulder, watching that matagot struggle to breathe.

I had hoped at least to catch a moment or two with Steph, but the night came and went without a sign of him anywhere in the Tower. The Wizard was in his library running five experiments at once. And to judge from the way he uncharacteristically snapped at me when I offered, he definitely didn't want any help.

So when morning came, I felt a little thick-headed from lack of sleep, and a lot lonely. Houdini once again refused to leave the bedside, and so I made my way alone to the Loose Leaves Teashop.

145

I could hear the sounds of Audrey in the back, pulling the last of her early morning baking out of the ovens. I took a moment to once more marvel at her energy, and feel a little guilty for how grumpy I was when I doubted she'd gotten any more sleep than I had.

But then I just turned towards our usual morning meetup table, and saw Liam was there, but not alone.

My brother Mercutio was with him.

He caught my eye at once and waved for me to join them. "Liam has just been catching me up on your latest case."

"Right," I said. I sat down, then looked over at Liam. "Audrey filled you in about our visit to Ursula?"

"Yeah. Sorry, it's another dead end. I can head upstairs and get back on the hunt for more leads," he offered. But then immediately made me feel guilty for even considering it when he yawned enormously.

"You should get some sleep," I said.

"No, I'm good!" he insisted. "I just need to get some of Audrey's tea in me. She's making me a pot of matcha. I'll be wide awake after that."

"And there's always that coffee place across the way," Mercutio said. "The Bitter Brew, right?"

"Right," I said to my brother, because that was indeed the name. But then I turned back to Liam. "But no. You'll only crash that much harder later, and you need your job. If there was anything else to be found, you'd have found it already. I just have to think of something else."

"Like what else?" Mercutio asked. He sounded genuinely curious.

"I don't know," I admitted, and slumped forward until my head hit the table with a smack.

"Audrey? Make that two pots of matcha," Mercutio called to the back of the teashop.

"What?" Audrey asked, popping her head out. Then she saw me lying there, face turned sideways so I could stare at her with bleary eyes. "Right. For Tabitha. On the way."

"Great. That means more of this Irish Breakfast is for me," Mercutio said, and filled his cup to the brim.

"It's just basic scones today," Audrey said as she brought a platter of the baked goods over to our table. "If you want them to be sweet, there's the jam. If you want them savory… I don't know." She slumped into the chair beside me, thoroughly defeated.

"This case really has you all down," Mercutio said. He split one of the scones, spread it with butter, then paused to think for a moment. With a whisper of an incantation, a little leather drawstring pouch appeared on his palm. He teased the top open, then pulled out a pinch of dried herbs and sprinkled them over his buttered scone. He reassembled the pieces, then took a bite off one corner.

"There," he said, his mouth still full. "Parsley, sage, rosemary, and thyme. Always a winning, and savory, combination. Any takers?"

The three of us just blinked at him like he wasn't speaking English.

"No? I'll just leave this here in case you change your minds," he said, and set the pouch beside the little jam jars.

"Matcha?" Liam said to Audrey.

"Oh, right," she said, and hoisted herself out of her chair to go fetch it.

"So why were you bothering to talk to Ursula Croft about any of this, anyway?" Mercutio asked between sips of tea. "The Croft family were noted herbalists, sure. But she's known largely for *not* being a noted herbalist."

"Huh?" I said, too tired to parse that sentence.

"She barely passed botany or potions classes in her academy days," Mercutio said, then took another bite of his now savory scone.

I frowned at him. "She's way older than us. No way was she still in school when you were."

"No, of course not. She just has a reputation. Mostly for unscrupulous manipulation of others."

Then he grinned at me. Audrey, who had just returned with a tray holding two pots of matcha, leaned close to my ear to say, "You know, it's just possible your brother might be able to help us. He could be our temporary Barnardo."

"I could never," Mercutio said. "I don't have anywhere near his number of opinions."

"But you know people. Like, a lot of people," I said. "Their reputations and histories and that. We don't need opinions about them, but facts like that last one are incredibly helpful."

"We don't really have much knowledge about the society scene," Audrey said.

"I think you'll find what I know more random than helpful, but I'll give it a shot if you want," Mercutio said with a shrug.

"I wish I knew what to even ask," I said, crumbling a scone onto my plate. As usual, strong caffeine was making me feel weird in a way where a little food in my belly would really help. But I had never felt less like eating in my life. So I was left with crumbs on my fingers and a growing queasiness in my belly.

"Barnardo Daley," Mercutio said musingly. "His father was a decent finance wizard back in his day. Too ethical to work for any of the major families. I guess that was how he ended up here, in the Square."

"You sound like this is some sort of backwater," Liam said.

Mercutio just shrugged. "It's not where finance wizards usually end up."

"It's not even where Barnardo wanted to be," I felt compelled to point out. "He only moved here because his father was ailing and needed his help. Before that, Barnardo was living downtown. I think in the Foshay Tower, even?"

I looked at Audrey, but she just shrugged.

"Never heard anything about his son, but Antonio Daley had a reputation for just making gold appear like... Well," he finished lamely.

"Like magic?" Liam asked, not quite mockingly.

"I mean," Mercutio said with another shrug.

"That was the matagot," I said. "Miss Snooty Cat. She must've been where the gold was coming from."

"Indeed," Mercutio said with an interested gleam to his eye. "Those are rare, and very hard to gain the trust of. That would explain the unusually early retirement. If you have a matagot, you don't really also need a job." He took a bite of his scone and chewed musingly, then said, "I guess that's Barnardo's secret, too. The matagot."

"He was running a successful business," I said.

"A decently successful small business," Liam said.

"Maybe the matagot was helping out with that," Mercutio said.

"Did Antonio make any enemies when he left the world of finance wizardry behind?" I asked. A total stab in the dark, but I had to ask.

"Doubtful," Mercutio said as he refilled his cup from the pot of Irish Breakfast tea. "Like I said, he was highly ethical. And as far as I know, he never ratted on anyone unethical. But if he had, I doubt that would blowback on Barnardo. Particularly not after so many years."

"Maybe we want to look into it a little more, anyway?" Audrey suggested.

"Wouldn't be any point," Mercutio put in before I could answer. "No, what you want to do is focus on Barnardo's enemies. I've been listening to him talk for weeks now. That man definitely has enemies in the plural."

"Maybe there are a few people who walk a different path to avoid talking with him. But no one could despise him to the point that they'd murder him," I said.

"Are you sure?" Mercutio asked.

"Well, maybe—" I started to say.

"No, we've suspected her twice before and been wrong both times," Audrey said before I could finish.

"And Cressida did tell us Cleopatra's not been to the salon for days. She's not been in the Square," I agreed with a sigh.

"Who's this?" Mercutio asked, buttering another scone.

I poked at the remains of my own scone scattered over my plate, then took another bracing sip of matcha. "Cleopatra Manx," I finally said when it became clear he wasn't going to stop staring at me until I answered.

"A Manx!" he said, slapping his hands together as if this piece of knowledge absolutely delighted him. "Come on, sis. You're not even eating. Let's go talk to her now."

"Oh, I'm so not in the mood for another conversation with Cleopatra Manx," I moaned.

"Tabitha," Audrey said chidingly.

"I know. It's the closest thing we have left to a lead," I said. "I just really hate talking to her."

"She can talk to me," Mercutio offered. "You can just feed me questions. Come on. I've been wanting to meet her, anyway."

"Why would you want to meet her?" I asked.

But before he could answer, I felt a familiar displacement of air behind me. I turned to see Steph, draped in the folds of the multi-colored cloak that aided his teleportation magic.

"Steph! I waited around the Tower all night, but you never came back," I said.

"Sorry," he said, sounding breathless. Then I noticed the dark smudges under his eyes, and the extra paleness to the rest of his already exceedingly pale skin.

"What's wrong?" I asked. "Houdini? Miss Snooty Cat?"

"No, it's Barnardo," he said. Liam and Audrey echoed my gasp, but Steph was already waving his hands at us in urgent negation. "No, he's fine! He's fine! More than fine. He's awake."

Then he held a hand out to me. "He wants to talk to you, Tabitha. Right away."

I nodded, scrambling out of my chair to all but lunge into his arms.

But as the folds of his robe fell around me and the taste of butter-scotch coated my tongue in the inexplicable way it always did when I was that close to Steph within the folds of that jewel-toned cloak, all I felt was consuming worry.

Barnardo being awake should be good news. So why was Steph's hurrying rush making me feel more than ever that Barnardo's time was about to run out?

CHAPTER
TWENTY

I must have been inside a hospital at some point in my life. I mean, presumably, I had been born in one. My birth certificate said so.

But since my memories didn't go further back than the day I started school, if I'd ever been hurt or sick enough as a little kid to need medical help, I didn't recall it. I had been to the infirmaries in various academies for different things. Mostly injuries after some accident with my out of control magic, but there had been a few common illnesses mixed in.

Still, it wasn't until I stepped out of the folds of Steph's multicolored cloak that I realized I had never actually given any thought as to what a magical hospital would look like. I had seen prosaic hospitals lots of times. Not in real life, only in films and shows, but still.

I don't know what exactly I was expecting, except maybe something like I'd seen in one of those medical shows.

But I did know I hadn't expected to find myself in the center of an operating theater. Like something the prosaics had used back in the 19th century, with wooden risers for observers to watch the proceedings.

Right beside where we were standing was an operating table made of heavy wood that reminded me instantly of Ursula Croft's butcher block kitchen table.

A table nearby held one of those porcelain jug and basin combos, currently clean and dry. Another table was covered in carefully arranged tools, a variety of scalpels, knives and bone saws.

But perhaps the most alarming thing was right beside my foot: a wooden box filled with sand. Not kitty litter. It could only be there to contain spills from the hapless soul spread out on that table.

"This is just for show," Steph said. I looked up at him and he almost grinned back, although I think he was a little too exhausted to pull that grin off. "The look on your face just now, like you were picturing Barnardo up on that table..." He ended with a shrug.

"Where are we exactly?" I asked. "I mean, I know it's the hospital, but—"

"This was once a wing of the medical school at the university," he said. "The prosaics started using it less and less after they built more modern facilities. I don't think they quite realize they never tore it down. We magic types just acquired it. We're underground, of course. But this room was indeed once used by doctors to demonstrate procedures to their students and other interested scholars."

I looked down at that box of sand and shuddered.

"Come on," Steph said. "I only brought us here to be sure we didn't try to teleport on top of someone. The patient rooms are this way."

He led me out a door at the back of the theater. We were definitely in a building from the 19th century, although one that looked very lovingly maintained. The walls were freshly painted, although the particular shade of green they favored was a bit dated. The wood pillars, doors and door and window frames were all brightly polished.

And everything smelled, not just clean, but pleasant. Like there was a garden in full bloom outside every window and a fresh breeze always blowing those scents through every room.

Only we were underground. So there was no garden outside those windows. Not really. Just a simple spell, much like the one Audrey used to keep her teashop filled with the cool air of the mountains of the Pacific Northwest even on the hottest, stickiest Midwestern days.

We passed through a large hall that was completely bare, although I could easily picture the Victorian era uses of the space: bed after bed in long rows as patients took the air coming in from those massive bay windows.

But past the hall were smaller rooms, and these were humming with the sounds of people coming and going. There were quiet conversations inside the rooms, or among clumps of a few people standing against the wall in the hallway. Most of them wore the deep sapphire blue tunics and robes of the magical medical practitioners.

Steph nudged my elbow, then pointed me to a room on my left. I nodded, then followed him into a nice-sized room that contained a single bed under a window that was magically porting in a single magnificent sunbeam. That sunbeam smelled like mesquite, like dry desert air.

But the intense warmth of its light made Barnardo lying there with his head on the pillow and his eyes closed look all the thinner and paler.

"Tabitha," Steph said softly. Not that I blamed him for whispering. There was some feeling in this place that was even stronger than what I had in libraries, that quiet was called for as much as possible.

"Yes?" I said, turning away from the heart-wrenching sight of Barnardo to look up at him.

"I have to go back to the Tower. Just for a few minutes. But I'll be back soon to bring you home again," he said.

"I can always catch a boat," I said.

"No, I'll be back," he said. But there was something about his face. Some new worry overlaid on the older worries.

"What is it?" I asked.

But he just shook his head. "I don't know for sure. Just a feeling. But I'll be back soon."

I nodded, then gave him a quick kiss. Then I turned back to Barnardo. I felt the shifting of the air pressure behind me as he disappeared, and my heart clenched a little.

But then Barnardo opened his eyes.

"Tabitha?" he asked, blinking as if he couldn't see beyond the reaches of that sunbeam.

"Barnardo, I'm here," I said, perching on the edge of his bed and taking his outstretched hand in both of mine. "I'm so glad to see you awake."

"I fade in and out," he said. Then he glanced over at the nightstand beside his bed. I was expecting something like another one of those porcelain jug and basin sets, or perhaps a phone or call button or something.

But the only thing on top of that 19th century wooden table was a single mushroom the size of an ottoman. Its stalk was an ivory white, but its cap was a bright emerald green, but dotted with growths that looked like pearls.

And it appeared to be breathing. The pillowy top was rising and falling, rising and falling.

In time to Barnardo's slow breathing.

"What does that do?" I asked, reaching out a hand but stopping before my fingertips quite brushed the surface. It looked like it was covered with sticky pollen, or maybe some kind of spores.

"It's watching over its children," Barnardo said. "Spores in my lungs. The spores are keeping me alive. Or so they tell me. I still feel like I'm dying."

"But you're awake now. Surely that means you're getting better?" I said.

"Maybe," Barnardo said. But it was very clear from his tone that he thought he was just humoring me. He didn't believe he was getting better at all.

And I felt worse than ever. I didn't need a dying man worrying about my feelings first.

"I've been trying to find out who did this to you, and how," I said, squeezing his hand in mine. "Mainly the how, so they can really make you better."

"I know," he said, reaching over with his far hand to pat both of mine. "They didn't even have to tell me that. I knew you would be."

"But so far, we've only dug up Troy McFarland and Ursula Croft, and we're pretty sure neither of them did this to you," I said.

Barnardo was quiet for so long I would think he'd fallen back asleep, save that his eyes were still open, if glassy.

But then he said, in the softest of whispers, "So you know about MacBeth's Marvels, then."

"Yeah. Sorry. I hope that doesn't make any trouble for you," I said with a wince.

"Nothing I wasn't asking for, I'm sure," he said. He seemed to collapse further into his pillow, like gravity had suddenly increased on his body. But then he looked at me, and his eyes were bright and wide awake. "It's not what you think, though. Troy is harmless. To me, anyway. I've done everything I could to keep him from trying to hurt others, but he's headstrong."

"Yeah, I got that impression," I said. "Steph had words with him, apparently."

"Ah," Barnardo said. "I would love to know what those words were."

"Sorry, I wasn't there," I said.

"Never mind," he said with a tired chuckle. "Ursula Croft, on the other hand, definitely wants to hurt me. Alas, she doesn't have the skills to cook an omelette, let alone trick me into consuming a rare magical poison without me detecting it."

There was something in the way he said the word *tricked* that stuck out to me. "You were on the lookout for poisons?" I asked, surprised. "Why? Has someone tried to do this before?"

"Yes," he said. "And I really wished I had told you and Audrey about it. But it was so easy to brush it off. The attempts were so very inept. A child in their first year of botany would've been instantly suspicious just by the smell."

"Something in your food?" I asked.

"My food? No, it was never *my* food," he said. And now he sounded angry, but an anger layered over a much deeper layer of sorrow. His voice was thick, but he forced the words out. "Never *my* food. No, it was always Miss Snooty Cat that was the target."

"Miss Snooty Cat?" I repeated. "But why? Because she's a matagot?"

"I don't know. Maybe," Barnardo said, but he sounded skeptical. "But very few people knew that's what she was. No, I think it was something else. Some other motive. Like maybe someone didn't want to kill me, they just wanted me to suffer."

"Because of MacBeth's Marvels?" I asked, still confused. That didn't link up with Miss Snooty Cat in any way I could see. But what did I know?

But Barnardo was shaking his head. "No, nothing to do with that. No, and I guess this is why I never told you and Audrey in the first place, because I knew what you would say."

"You think it was Cleopatra Manx," I guessed.

He didn't answer me, didn't even nod. But I could tell by the fire in his eyes that I had hit the mark.

Only, it still didn't make sense. "Cressida said Cleopatra hasn't been in the salon for days. I don't know where she was, at home or on vacation. But not in the Square, presumably. But even if she had been, why would she do that? Why would she try to kill Miss Snooty Cat to get at you? I know the two of you really dislike each other, but it's a pretty big leap from that to killing your cat."

"I'm sure it was her," Barnardo said. "I feel it in my bones."

Then he closed his eyes and sunk further into that pillow again.

"Mercutio wanted to go talk to her," I said. "We were just about to do that when Steph brought me here to see you."

"I'm sorry I interrupted, then," Barnardo said, but it was like all the fire had gone out of him. Now he was just ash, about to be puffed away on the first hint of a breeze.

"We don't have any evidence that points to her," I said. "I'll talk to her, but I can't make any promises."

He nodded, but his eyes remained closed.

Then the mushroom on the side table suddenly gave an enormous shudder. A cloud of that sticky pollen broke free from its surface, floating into the air to dance like dust motes in the sunbeam. But the mushroom still kept shaking.

Could fungi have seizures?

I heard the sounds of feet racing down the hall outside the door, heading towards our room. I leaned closer to Barnardo, but as far as I could tell, he was breathing as slowly and evenly as ever.

I stepped back out of the way as the medical staff burst into the room, rushing to his bedside. One woman in full sapphire robes focused her attention on the mushroom, wheeling the table on its casters a little way away from the bedside before passing her hands over its trembling surface.

"Is he okay?" I asked as I shrank back against the wall, desperate to stay out of the way.

A man wearing his sapphire tunic over prosaic jeans was waving what looked like a tuning fork over Barnardo's prostrate form. He seemed to be listening, but I could hear no sound save the murmurs from conversations trickling in from other rooms.

Then he put the fork away and looked up at me as if he hoped I had the answer to some puzzle.

"He just took a turn," the woman across from him said, although whether to him or me, I wasn't sure. She was leaning in closely, her hands on either side of Barnardo's face, gazing at his flickering eyelids as he slept.

"For the better?" I asked.

"Yes," she said. Then she looked up at the younger man in the jeans. "His immune system just rallied?"

"But that makes no sense," he said. "I've only seen this in wizards with familiars. And he insisted that cat wasn't his familiar."

"So Miss Snooty Cat is awake and making him well?" I asked.

I felt a hand on my arm and realized that Steph was back already, having just stepped into the room from the hallway. I smiled up at him, but the smile froze on my face.

Before I could ask him what had happened, the man in the jeans went on. "No, I really don't think so. No, when I've seen this in the past, it's when a familiar gives up its life. The sudden surge of shared life force back into the witch looks like this."

I looked to Steph for confirmation, desperately hoping I'd see him shaking his head.

But he didn't. He just looked exhausted. And sad.

"Miss Snooty Cat?" I asked.

"She passed," Steph said. "She never woke up."

"But Barnardo is going to be okay?" I asked, shifting my gaze from Steph to the medical team.

The man in jeans was chewing at his lip in thought, but after a glance to the woman across from him, he just shook his head.

"He's rallied some strength. He can keep fighting the poison for a little while longer. But if we don't identify the poison and counteract it, we've just bought a little more time is all."

A little more time. I couldn't waste a moment of it.

And yet, there was still something I had to do first.

"Steph, take me to Houdini?" I asked.

"Of course," he said.

Then those folds of robes were around me once more, and we were on our way back to the Tower.

TWENTY-ONE

Steph brought us straight to the Wizard's fireplace in the library. There was a crackling fire burning there, filling the air with the smell of applewood and fragrant smoke.

A little *too* fragrant. I knew a calming formula when I smelled it.

But knowing what it was didn't make it any less effective. As soon as I had taken a breath, some of the tightness in my chest started to fade away. After two breaths, I no longer felt like some monstrous fist was squeezing my heart.

After three breaths, I was ready to step away from Steph, towards where Houdini was waiting, curled up tight on the Wizard's lap. He watched me approach with his big brown eyes, then sat up and leaned toward me as I bent to scoop him up into my arms.

"I'm so sorry, Houdini," I said. "I'm so sorry that after all that waiting by her side, you didn't even get a chance to say goodbye."

"I said goodbye," he said in my mind. His face was buried against the side of my neck. I could feel the droop of his ears against my jaw, and his tail hung limply over my arm.

"It was good that you were there, even if she didn't know it," I said.

"No, she knew," he said. Then he pushed away from my shoulder to look up into my face. "I saw her."

"But Steph said she didn't wake up?" I said.

"No, she never did," Houdini said.

"She used the last of her magic to pull him into a world that only existed in her mind," the Wizard said softly. "Only for a moment, and then she was gone. But I gather it was enough."

"Did she tell you anything? About you, I mean," I asked Houdini.

"No, it wasn't about that," he said, and laid his head against my neck again. "We just had a moment where we finally really understood each other. I wished we'd had that sooner."

"Barnardo is still poisoned," I said to the Wizard as I stroked Houdini's back. "We still haven't solved this."

"No," he said, and planted his hands on the arms of his chair to leverage himself up onto his feet. "There is much work to be done, and we're running out of time to do it."

"But we know Barnardo's company, MacBeth's Marvels, isn't the reason for any of this," I said.

"Perhaps not," the Wizard said, brushing the wrinkles from the front of his robes. "But what he was selling was certainly interesting."

"Magic?" I asked, and braced myself for his answer.

Barnardo would be in so much trouble if the answer was yes.

"Not... exactly," the Wizard said.

"What does that mean?" I asked.

"There is some magic in the liquid within those bottles, but it's not *magic* magic," he said.

"Huh?" was all I managed in response.

"I've lived for quite some time, as you well know. But even for me, this is something rarely seen. Magic from a prosaic," he said. "It has a distinctive flavor to how a magical person perceives it. It's magic, but not really."

"But Barnardo isn't a prosaic," I said.

"No, of course not," the Wizard said. "Which makes it all so very curious. And the legal ramifications extra puzzling. I will have much to discuss with him, when this is all safely resolved."

"Right," I said. There was still a poisoner to catch first. "You know, Barnardo is convinced that Cleopatra Manx was the one who did it."

"I know he didn't like her, but that still sounds like a big leap," Steph said. "I know they didn't get along, but murder is a lot."

"That's the thing. He thinks she was trying to kill Miss Snooty Cat, not him," I said.

"And she succeeded," the Wizard said, stroking his beard ponderously. Then he realized both Steph and I were gaping at him and added, "If she did it, that is."

"Does she have the skills to do it?" I asked. I thought rhetorically, but the Wizard answered at once.

"Oh, definitely," he said. "Not that she'd need to. More than her own considerable skills, she has wealth. That opens many windows of opportunity."

"Barnardo said it had happened before," I said. "Someone tried to poison Miss Snooty Cat before. He didn't tell me when or how, or even exactly how many times. He just said they were easily detected."

"As if someone were hiring out for the job and after each failure hired a progressively more skilled recruit?" Steph said.

"Or in the end, she took matters into her own hands," the Wizard said.

"I don't like accusing someone with absolutely no proof," I said. "I suppose Audrey and I could go over to her salon and do our poison detecting spell. That might turn up something. But in all likelihood, she cooked up this poison at home. If she did it at all."

"She'll let you into her home," Steph said.

"You sound awfully sure," I said.

"Well, it would be awkward not to. Your brother is there right now," he said.

"What?"

"He left the teashop after we did, but he didn't go out the prosaic door. He went into the Square, then up to the top floor apartments," Steph said.

"Wait," I said, pressing a hand to my suddenly pounding head. "Who told you this?"

"Audrey," he said.

"When did you talk to Audrey?" I asked.

"Before I came back for you," he said. "She was calling for me."

"Why?" I asked.

"To tell me about Mercutio," he said. "Apparently it's a little odd for him to go inside the Square."

"Yeah, a little," I agreed. "But why did he go to the third floor apartments if he wanted to see Cleopatra? Doesn't she live in the Foshay Tower?"

"She has a condo in Manhattan, actually, not in the Foshay Tower. But lately she's been spending more time in the Square," Steph said.

I knew he kept tabs on everyone inside the Square. He and the Wizard maintained all the magic that kept us apart from the prosaic world, that kept us safe. Part of doing that was knowing when magical people came and left.

Still, it felt a little creepy how quickly he just knew that.

"How long is lately?" I asked.

"She moved into the open apartment on the third floor over the comic shop about two weeks ago," he said with a shrug.

"That's kind of close to Barnardo's place," I said.

"Is it? He's a bit further south, and down a level," Steph said.

"Still, I wished I'd asked Barnardo more questions. Like whether these poison attempts started before or after she moved in here," I said. "Do you know why she's here?"

"I only know she hasn't left the Square in that time," he said. "No trips to Mallorca, no shopping in Paris. Nothing."

"She is down a person in her salon, but that's been true for a while," I said. "But even if that's why she's decided to move closer—

setting aside that with her portal traveling capabilities, nothing is much of a commute for her—she's not been in the salon at all. And Cressida didn't know where she was. If Cleopatra had moved upstairs and Cressida knew about it, she would've said so. I know she would have."

"Let me take Houdini," Steph said, and I passed the little dog over to his arms. It felt a lot like trading off baby tending duties. Houdini didn't stir, just pressed his face against the side of Steph's neck as readily as he had done with mine.

Poor little guy. He was beyond exhausted.

"Audrey was prepping more poison detecting bottles for the spell when I saw her. Go get her and knock on Cleopatra's door while Mercutio is still there. You can always pretend you were looking for him and not rouse her suspicions," Steph said.

"Unless Mercutio has roused them already," I said with a sigh. I really didn't like the idea of my brother muddling up my investigation. Even though I wasn't in any position of authority or anything. He was as free as I was to ask people questions, after all.

But I didn't quite understand why he wanted to.

Or what he had meant when he'd said he'd been wanting to meet her, anyway. He had never told me why. Was he just looking for a networking opportunity with a member of one of the oldest, richest, and most powerful magical families in the New World?

"Call me if you need me," Steph said as he planted a quick kiss on my cheek. "Houdini and I are just going to be here in the laboratory, testing an infinite number of potential poisons."

"Right," I said. As if I needed to be reminded that Barnardo's clock was still ticking.

I closed my eyes and imagined the smell of tea and scones.

But nothing happened.

A surge of butterscotch taste on my tongue ruined my efforts to recall my sense memories of the teashop. But it was just Steph, moving closer to kiss my cheek again. Just like the Wizard had tapped my shoulder before.

Then I opened my eyes, and I was in the Loose Leaves Teashop.

As if she had known I was coming, Audrey was already locking the prosaic door and turning her sign to *closed*.

"Did you know Cleopatra was living in the Square full-time?" I asked Audrey without preamble.

"No. But I find it strange that Barnardo didn't tell us. He must have known," she said. She picked up a green glass bottle from a row of similar bottles behind her counter then walked with me towards the Square door.

"It seems like there were a couple of things that Barnardo wasn't telling us," I said. And as we climbed all the stairs to the third floor, I told her about the previous poisoning attempts.

"I'm sorry about Miss Snooty Cat, I really am," Audrey said when we'd reached the last of the steps and followed the cast-iron walkway towards the newly tenanted apartment over the comic shop.

"But?" I said, because Audrey's voice had had that tone to it.

"But, it's not like she went out of her way to be likable at all," Audrey said. "Still, it feels weird, imagining someone hating her so much they tried to kill her. As far as I know, she never left Barnardo's apartment, except for when she was with Barnardo. And Cleopatra's dislike seemed pretty focused on Barnardo. Why bring his cat into it?"

"But she wasn't a cat," I said.

"We only just found that out," she reminded me. "And it doesn't seem like it's common knowledge. Like, at all."

"Even if you knew she was a matagot, why kill her, though?" I said. "What is there to be gained in that?"

Audrey sighed, tapping the empty bottle against her palm. But in the end, she could only answer me with a shrug.

I took a deep breath, then knocked on the door.

I could hear voices inside, a masculine and a feminine one. The feminine one was low and sultry, too low for the words to carry through the door.

But the masculine one was louder. I heard my brother saying, "If that's true, why didn't he tell me? Why tell you?"

I shot Audrey a questioning glance, but she didn't understand it either.

Cleopatra's sultry voice was still indistinguishable through the door, but the click of her heels grew louder as she came towards us. Audrey wrapped both of her hands around the green bottle, not quite hiding it but making it a little less obvious.

Then the door swung open and Cleopatra stood there, smiling down at us with that smile that was something other than friendly. I'm not sure what that smile was meant to convey, but it always sent tickles of apprehension up my spine.

Not that Cleopatra wasn't conventionally beautiful. She was practically the Platonic ideal of a certain kind of beauty. Her long blonde hair was so expertly treated it looked naturally sun-kissed, to match her perfectly bronzed skin. Her curves were shown to best advantage by the cut of her spaghetti-strapped minidress with its plunging neckline. And her eyes were a very memorable shade of bluish-green, a shade I had never seen in any other set of eyes ever in my life.

But more than that, she had a way of walking, or even just standing, that radiated elegance and grace. She was like a living icon of old school Hollywood.

She even smelled really, really good.

It was a shame she was unpleasant, manipulative, maybe even downright evil.

"Tabitha Greene and Audrey Mirken, whatever are you doing on my doorstep?" she asked in almost a coo.

"I'm looking for my brother," I said. Why was my throat so suddenly dry? It wasn't like there wasn't enough moisture in the air.

Then I felt a sudden stab of panic, wondering what a disaster show my hair must be by now. Because of course Cleopatra was looking at it. Looking at it with that expression on her face that said she would be wrinkling her nose in disgust, if only that wouldn't risk those wrinkles becoming permanent.

"You have a brother?" she asked. "That's the first I've heard of it. I thought those bookshop husbands were your only family."

I decided it would be best not to engage with *that* at all. Instead, I leaned closer to the doorframe to try to look around her.

"Mercutio?" I called.

There was the scrape of chair legs on tiled floor, then my brother appeared in the doorway between the entryway and the kitchen.

"Oh, hey, sis," he said casually.

"Hey? That's all you have to say to me?" I asked.

But Cleopatra had turned to look at Mercutio, her eyes sweeping over him as if seeing him for the first time.

Then she turned back to me with that same not quite wrinkling the nose look on her face.

"Yeah, he's my brother," I said, folding my arms.

"But you said your name was Mercutio Ward, darling," Cleopatra said to him, that coo back in her voice.

"That's right," he said, rubbing at the back of his neck as if her question made him uncomfortable.

Cleopatra looked us both over a second time. Then she said, "Different fathers?"

"No, same parents," I said.

"I have our father's name. Tabitha has our mother's," Mercutio said. He looked like admitting that was embarrassing him a little.

But I'm sure all Cleopatra was noticing in that moment was that the flush of color to his otherwise pale skin only made him that much more attractive. Indeed, she was licking her lips slowly. Like my brother was some succulent main course.

"It's really not that strange," I said.

Then Cleopatra turned to look at me again. Only this look was far more intense than before. She leaned in close enough that her breath fogged my glasses, and I took them off to clean them with the hem of my T-shirt.

But still she looked at me, like she'd never really seen me before.

"So you're a Ward," she said. Slowly, as if that piece of information answered so many questions.

"I really prefer Greene," I told her. Then I put my glasses back on and gave the frames an adjusting twist. Just like my uncle always did.

Cleopatra smirked. But she stepped back from the door. "Please, child of the Ward family. Make yourself at home."

I stood there stupidly for a moment, but Audrey nudged me hard. I remembered why we were there and accepted Cleopatra's invitation with a nod, stepping into her sitting room that was just as elegant and just as cold as the woman herself.

Mercutio looked amused, but followed my lead, choosing one of the other white leather club chairs to sink down into. As always, he looked like a pirate lord sprawled on the throne of the king he'd just deposed, swaggeringly casual. He even tossed his long hair back as he looked at Cleopatra.

She seemed to need a moment to collect herself. But then that smile was back, and she closed the door before settling on the very edge of the chair between mine and Mercutio's.

Then she looked at Mercutio, and he met her gaze with those icy blue eyes of his. They seemed locked together with an intensity that was really uncomfortable for me, also sitting there.

But it did mean that Audrey slipped into the kitchen without anyone but me noticing.

One way or another, we were going to get some answers.

There was no way I was leaving this apartment without them.

CHAPTER
TWENTY-TWO

Cleopatra was still gazing intently at my brother. And didn't seem likely to stop anytime soon.

I cleared my throat. Loudly.

Mercutio glanced over at me questioningly. As if he had no idea why I had just done that.

"I interrupted a conversation between the two of you," I said.

"Did you? Oh, that was nothing," Cleopatra said with a little wave that made the gold bangles on her wrist tinkle musically together. "Just small talk."

"I *was* trying to talk to her about Barnardo," Mercutio said to me with just a hint of defensiveness in his tone. "I wasn't sure how long you'd be at the hospital, so I decided to come up here without you."

"You knew Cleopatra was up here?" I asked.

"You were at the hospital? I do hope you're all right," Cleopatra said with too precise of timing. Like she wanted to pretend that we'd both started talking at once, but clearly she was redirecting before Mercutio could answer my question.

"She went to see Barnardo," Mercutio said to her. So her little redirect had been successful. For now.

"And how is he?" Cleopatra asked, propping her chin on her hand and looking at me with those empirically gorgeous eyes.

"Not well," I said. "He's been poisoned."

"We all know that," she said, then quickly added, "such a pity. And a crime. I meant, has there been any change in his condition?"

"He was awake," Mercutio said. His quick responses to her questions were starting to irritate me. But I could hear the murmur of Audrey's voice coming from the kitchen. She was casting the spell. And from the kitchen, she could easily slip deeper into the apartment without anyone in the sitting room noticing.

Provided I kept them just a little bit distracted.

"His body is still fighting the poison. The magical medical practitioners can't do more than slow the rate of its effects until we know what poison was used," I said. "But his timeline was extended by a bit just a short while ago."

"That is good news. How did they accomplish that?" Cleopatra asked, and blinked at me in a way I'm sure she thought was quite winning a gesture.

She was playing innocent. But she wasn't doing a very polished job of it. I was starting to think it was deliberate, that shortfall in her acting skills.

But why?

"How did they?" Mercutio asked, genuinely curious.

"They didn't," I said. "Miss Snooty Cat gave up her own fight and passed the last of her life force over to Barnardo."

"She could do that? I thought she wasn't his familiar," Mercutio said.

"She was something far more," Cleopatra said. Then her cheeks turned ever so slightly pink as she sat back in her chair and uncrossed then recrossed her legs. Like she hadn't intended to say that out loud.

"You knew what she was?" I asked.

"Not a cat?" Cleopatra said. Not quite a question.

"I'll repeat my question. Did you know what she was?" I asked again.

Cleopatra licked her lips ever so slowly, playing for time. Then she gave me a dazzling smile, leaning forward with a gleam in her eyes like whatever she said next was going to be truly devastating.

But the smile froze on her lips, and the gleam faded from her eyes, as she saw Audrey suddenly standing behind me. In one hand, she held the glowing green bottle she had used as a vessel for our poison detecting spell.

And in the other she held a small brown bottle, the kind people kept essential oils in which was currently also glowing a sickening shade of green.

There was a picture of a sprig of lavender on the faded label of that little bottle. But I was pretty sure when the Wizard was done testing it, there wasn't going to be more than a hint of lavender to the contents within.

"It looks like it's confession time," Mercutio said to Cleopatra.

Cleopatra licked her lips slowly again, but I could see the thoughts racing behind her nervous eyes.

But the last thing I was going to do now was to let her play for more time.

Because it wasn't her time she was looking to play with. It was Barnardo's.

"Audrey, get that to the Wizard at once," I said. "Just think of him and the Tower, and you'll be there."

She nodded, but I could tell from the way she glanced down at her hands that she regretted they were both full and she couldn't tuck the hair behind her ears first. She just clutched the bottles tightly, then closed her eyes.

And vanished in a wink.

I turned back to Cleopatra. "It's only a matter of time now. Barnardo will recover. And you'll be in prison. But I'm here if you want to rant a little about how I foiled your plans first."

"Oh, I doubt very much I'll see the inside of a prison cell, dear," she said, folding her arms and sinking back into her chair.

"Yeah, with her family's money, it will likely be house arrest," Mercutio said.

I glared at him, not sure why he was putting that thought out there. Was he even trying to help?

But then he went on, speaking to Cleopatra, "Like your Uncle Tybalt and your Aunt Hermia. They've been under house arrest for nearly fifty years. Have you even met them?"

"When I was a girl," Cleopatra said coldly.

"Leading fulfilling lives, are they?" Mercutio asked.

Cleopatra did that lip licking thing again, but had no sharp comeback to his words.

"Do you want to tell me why you did it?" I asked. I tried to sound soft and empathetic. I think I got most of the way there.

But she just said, "No," without quite meeting my eyes.

"It will all come out in court," Mercutio said. He sounded like everything going on was somehow amusing to him. He tended to sound like that a lot, but in that moment I found it irritating. Inappropriate.

Then Cleopatra burst out with, "It's not like it's even against magic law."

"Murder?" I asked, flabbergasted.

"Murder? The thing was a matagot. If anything, it's monster slaying. A time-honored profession. The best monster slayers were awarded titles and estates, back in the day," she said.

"Back in the day," Mercutio said musingly.

"You tried to kill Barnardo," I pointed out. "Hopefully, now that we have your poison, he can be cured. But even so, that's attempted murder. That's absolutely against the law."

"How was I supposed to know he'd go sipping his kitty-cat's cream?" she asked. "I was very careful. He had two containers of cream in his shopping bag when he came back from the farmers' market, the large one for him and the small one for Miss Snooty Cat. He even told Octavia Abergavenny that when he added his shopping from her store to the same bag. He always buys a large one for him and a small one for her. She told me so herself, because I asked. I made sure. It's not my fault he's so greedy he steals sips from his own cat."

She sounded for all the world like some of the students I had known back in my academy days, the ones that wanted to argue every point on every test with the professor. Like she shouldn't be docked points for how she executed that part of her assassination plot.

"You knew she wasn't a cat. Somehow, I don't think you tried to kill her because you were hoping for titles and estates to be awarded to you as a monster slayer," I said.

"No one's done that in years," Mercutio put in.

"Why did you kill her?" I asked.

But Cleopatra just crossed her arms more firmly, sank further back into her club chair, and pressed her lips tightly together.

She had no intention of answering my question.

And she still hadn't said a word when, a quarter of an hour later, the authorities arrived to arrest her.

"She's probably right about the house arrest, you know," Mercutio said to me as we stood on the cast-iron balcony and watched her being led away. "She's not even wrong about the lack of crime in killing Miss Snooty Cat."

"I guess it's just her bad luck that Barnardo was nearly killed as well," I said crossly. "Now she can't get away with it. Not entirely."

We followed behind the arresting team, down all the flights of stairs to the ground floor. A crowd was already starting to gather there, standing in ones and twos, silently watching Cleopatra being led into the pub. She was one short boat ride away from being in a jail cell, even if only for as long as it took for her family to get her back out again.

I saw Cressida Cade standing at the edge of the crowd, watching her boss leave through the one route she had never chosen as a free woman. Cleopatra had always jumped through the portal at the heart of the hedge maze, whisking away to far more glamorous destinations than could be reached by the underground boat system.

When I had first come to the Square, the Inanna Salon & Spa had been run by all three members of the Trio. But Delilah had been killed and now Cleopatra was never coming back again. Even if she got away with house arrest and never saw the inside of a prison cell, as she claimed, she would also never see the inside of her own business again.

Now Cressida Cade stood alone.

As if she sensed me looking at her, she met my eyes briefly. But her face was inscrutable as she slowly turned away and went back inside the salon doors.

I might have been imagining it, but I thought I detected a slight spring to her step as she did so, though. Her future suddenly had a lot more opportunities for her. And knowing Cressida, she would explore them all.

I looked up at Mercutio, who was still gazing at the closed door to the pub.

"What were you two talking about when I knocked on the door?" I asked.

"Hm?" he said as if he hadn't heard me. But I knew he had.

"You said something about if something was true, why didn't 'he' tell you? Who's 'he'?" I asked.

He frowned at me in puzzlement. Then something clicked in his mind and he said, "Oh! Right. We were talking about Barnardo."

"So what truth didn't he tell you?" I asked.

"Hm?" he said again, again like he hadn't quite heard me. But the crowd around us was barely murmuring to each other. The loudest sound was the buzz of bees in the orchard, and that was scarcely loud at all.

"Mercutio," I said in my sternest voice.

"Honestly, it was nothing," he said. Then his cheeks flushed with color. "To be honest, it was such a relief when you knocked on that door. It was a mistake, me going there alone. I had no idea how... forceful she was going to be."

"Forceful," I repeated skeptically.

"She was aggressively flirty," he said. "Not something I normally mind, but not really what I'm looking for when dealing with a murder suspect."

"I think we can just call her a murderer now," I said. "Technicality be damned. Miss Snooty Cat might not have been beloved by all, but she was beloved by Barnardo. What Cleopatra did was absolutely a crime."

"I agree," Mercutio said.

We walked back to the teashop in companionable silence. But I just couldn't shake the feeling that he wasn't being totally honest with me. Even though he'd just used that very word twice.

"You're sure it was Barnardo you were talking about when I overheard you?" I asked again as we stood at the door out to the prosaic world, and to Mercutio's walk home to the apartment he shared with Liam.

"Absolutely," he said. He started to unlock the door, but then turned back to look at me again. "Just out of curiosity, who did you think I was talking about?"

"I don't know," I said, and I could feel my cheeks flushing hotly.

"Tabitha," he said chidingly.

"I thought, maybe, it was about our father," I said.

"Why would you think that?" he asked, a little furrow of worry appearing between his perfect eyebrows.

"You wanted to see Cleopatra because she was a Manx, right? And you're a Ward, just like our father," I said.

"You're a Ward too," he reminded me.

"You really weren't talking about him?" I asked.

He sighed, then took me by both shoulders, looking me straight in the eyes. "Tabitha, I've told you, I've never actually met our father," he said. "It would be pretty strange for me to ask Cleopatra, whom I'd just met, why if something was true our father didn't tell me, when I've never spoken to him in my life. Wouldn't you agree?"

"Yeah," I said.

It sounded like the truth. And his eyes were absolutely sincere.

But after he'd left and I'd locked the door again behind him, I still had a gnawing feeling in my gut that it wasn't the whole truth.

I remembered the pressure on my mind I had felt while at Troy McFarland's place, so familiar from when the same thing had happened in Geneva.

But also so familiar when I had felt it in Geneva for what had surely been the first time.

I had known that presence. But I couldn't recall it.

It only made sense that who I had felt had been someone I had known before my memories began. Someone from my young childhood.

Someone like my father.

I felt the silver bracelet on my wrist thrum. It wasn't asking if I wanted to access to my power. But it did feel like a gentle warning.

I ignored it. I closed my eyes and mentally called out a name. I did it softly, with nothing like the excess of power I had used when I had needed Steph's help in a fight for my life against the man who had murdered Delilah Dare. It was just a gentle mental whisper.

Only it wasn't Steph's name I was calling out to.

"Benvolio Ward?" I whispered.

Yeah, I might've said it out loud too. But it didn't matter. I was alone in the darkened teashop.

But suddenly the world around me was full, too full, with an awesome sense of presence.

It was the sensation from before, from in Geneva, but multiplied a thousandfold.

I don't know if there were ever going to be any words of answer emerging from that overwhelming sense of presence. I waited and waited as it built and built until I found myself trembling on the teashop's tiled floor. Like that presence was pushing me down to the ground.

I managed one more whispered word, a simple, "Dad?"

Then the world went black.

TWENTY-THREE

I tasted butterscotch on my tongue, rich and sweet, melting and oozing over every taste receptor in my mouth, and I knew I was no longer alone.

Then an arm was under my shoulders, hoisting me up to a sitting position, and that momentary warm and cozy dream of butterscotch jarred back into a far too sensory nightmare.

My head was splitting in the worst headache I'd ever had in my life. It was like my skull was physically coming apart, like all the muscles of my scalp were spasming as they tried to hold it together, like the blood vessels were throbbing hotly in an effort to keep the supply coming.

The ringing in my ears had two tones, a high-pitched shriek that waxed and waned over a steady background of ominous humming.

My sense of smell and taste were both overwhelmed by the presence of rancid butter in my mouth. I could feel the oily graininess of it on my tongue. It was horrid, made all the more so for being a perversion of my favorite thing in the world.

I couldn't get my eyes open enough to see anything, which was probably a blessing. Every time I tried, the first hint of light redoubled the pain in my head and I scrunched them back shut again.

The only good sensation in all of that was the arm around my shoulders. It tightened around me. At first I thought someone was trying to pick me up, but then my stomach started doing somersaults and I realized that while I was still sitting on the floor, it was no longer the cool tiles of the teashop beneath me.

It was the thickly woven but worn carpet that covered the floor before the fireplace in the Wizard's library.

Now two people were fussing around me, although I couldn't pinpoint quite who they were. It had to be the Wizard and Steph, but I couldn't open my eyes to see them or even hear them over the cacophony roaring in my ears.

I just wanted to curl up on the floor and hug my knees and wait for it all to be over.

And I really hoped that wasn't the same thing as wanting to die, but for a fraction of a moment, I was willing to take that risk.

Then a new sensation broke through everything. A warm, furry little body was on my lap. Paws were planted on my chest and a little tongue was licking all over my face, anxiously and relentlessly.

I put out my hands to push him away, but the feel of his fur on my skin was too much of a comfort. I couldn't hug him—his whole body was trembling with the effort of keeping that licking going—but just touching his sides was enough.

Finally, the sound of his voice in my mind broke past the ringing of my ears and the force of that headache.

"Tabitha! Tabitha! Tabitha!"

"I'm fine, Houdini," I said, but my tongue felt thick in my mouth, and I wasn't sure how clear any of those sounds came out.

"Here," someone else said. It was someone speaking out loud, and their voice was barely making it through the shrieking and humming that droned on and on, but I thought it was the Wizard.

Then Houdini was moved aside and a mug of something warm and sharp smelling was thrust against my lips. Just inhaling the smell started to clear my mind a little. Ginger. Turmeric. Black pepper?

But when I drank it down, those spices were overwhelmed by the stickiness of an enormous quantity of honey. It was hard to swallow, it was so thick.

Then something else was in my face, not a dog or a mug of beverage. It was something with a strongly pungent smell, stronger than ammonia.

But it cleared the last of the clouds out of my head. I could finally open my eyes and see that I was, indeed, sitting on the carpet inside the library in the Tower.

And Steph was kneeling next to me, holding Houdini so tightly the word "restraining" might be more apt.

And the Wizard was crouching before me, a small brown glass vial pinched between two fingertips. He retracted it the moment my eyes sprung open, corking it and slipping it away in a pocket.

"What was that?" I grumbled, but he just thrust the mug in my hands up to my mouth again.

I took another long swallow of the spiced honey.

"How are you feeling?" the Wizard asked. "Be specific."

I nodded, then took a quick self inventory. "My head is still feeling a little sore, but the splitting headache has passed. My ears have stopped ringing. That honey got the bad taste out of my mouth. I feel exhausted, like I just ran a marathon or something, and I'm probably trembling more than Houdini over there. But I'm okay."

The Wizard just looked at me, like he didn't think my answer had been thorough enough.

I swallowed hard and tried to figure out what he was still looking for. "I don't feel that presence on my mind anymore. I think it's passed on."

"You felt it before," the Wizard said. Not a question.

I nodded.

"Of course she did," Steph said, his voice muffled, as he was nuzzling Houdini's neck at the same time. But his eyes when they met mine were as angry as I had ever seen them.

"You felt it too?" I asked. Although I had no idea why that would make him so angry with me.

The Wizard pondered carefully before answering. "We did not. But we did hear you call out to your father."

"Why, Tabitha? Why would you do that?" Steph asked. He was definitely angry at me.

But, like the Wizard would do, I thought my response through before I answered. "Some things were bothering me. Not just with the investigation. Things with my brother were bothering me. I can't point to anything specific, but I suddenly had the sensation that all these puzzles were missing the same piece. And comparing the puzzles, I knew just what the piece was."

"Your father?" Steph asked, skeptically.

"I wasn't aware he had any connection to Barnardo at all," the Wizard said with a frown.

But that snapped my attention in another direction entirely. "Barnardo! The poison!"

"Audrey brought it to us," the Wizard assured me. "The magical medical practitioners have it. They will administer the antidote the moment they have it brewed up. He will have a long, slow recovery, but he will recover."

"Thank goodness," I said. I was so relieved it was almost like I melted down into the carpet as the constant tension of the last few days finally evaporated.

But also, that exhaustion was making the idea of becoming a puddle in front of the library fire really tempting.

"Your father?" Steph asked again.

"They've arrested Cleopatra Manx," I said.

"We heard," the Wizard said, nodding.

"She wasn't trying to kill Barnardo. She was trying to kill Miss Snooty Cat. She won't say why, but I'm sure in my bones she was doing it at someone else's command," I said.

They both just looked at me, waiting for me to continue.

I licked my lips nervously. "Miss Snooty Cat is a matagot. She's also... *was* also highly intelligent and educated. She knew things about Houdini, or rather had ways to find out what she wanted to know about Houdini. I think she could do the same about anything that struck her fancy."

"You think Cleopatra killed her because of something she knew?" Houdini asked.

"No," I said slowly. "I think more she just wanted to remove Miss Snooty Cat *before* she could figure something out."

"She will be questioned by the authorities, of course," the Wizard said. But he gave me a grave frown. "She will almost certainly refuse to tell them anything. And with someone of her innate magical talents, there is very little anyone can do to compel her to speak when she chooses not to."

"She moved into the Square some time ago. I don't think she did that because she wanted a change of scenery. I think she was more... paving the way for someone else," I said.

"Just a hunch?" Steph asked me.

"Unfortunately, yes. Just a hunch," I said. "But that's why I wanted to talk to my father."

"You think he's coming to the Square?" the Wizard asked.

"I think he's the one who keeps trying to intrude on my mind," I said. "I think he found me quite by accident in Geneva, but he knew who I was at once. And now he found me in Minneapolis, only this time on purpose. I was just trying to see if he was still close by or not. That's why I called out."

"What you're failing to take into account is the uncontrolled, overpowered nature of your magic," Steph said. "That little call of yours would carry around the entire globe. He wouldn't have to be near to hear it."

"I was too loud again?" I asked. At least I hadn't blown out my voice this time. I was getting a smidge more control.

"Did he answer you?" the Wizard asked.

"Not in words. Not even just to say my name," I said, surprised to find that admitting as much actually made me feel a little sad.

"You felt the pressure of his presence on your mind again, like before?" the Wizard asked.

"Not like before," I said, almost in a moan. "I mean, it was familiar like that. But it was way more intense. And then I was unconscious. And then I wasn't unconscious, I only wished I still were."

"You're lucky Steph found you as quickly as he did," the Wizard said sternly. "The damage to your psyche was well on its way to becoming permanent."

"Seriously?" I asked, pressing my fingertips to my temples.

It had felt bad. But permanent damage bad?

I shivered.

"Do you think he's in town because Tabitha is here?" Steph asked the Wizard. He was still nuzzling Houdini's neck, but which of the two of them found it more comforting in that moment was likely a toss-up.

"Ah, but both of his children are in town, aren't they?" the Wizard mused.

"Mercutio went to see Cleopatra without me," I said. "He wanted to meet her, he had said just this morning. He says it's because she's from a prominent family. But that doesn't feel like the answer to me."

"Do you trust your brother?" the Wizard asked me.

I really wished I had a dog in my arms so I could bury my face in his fur. Without it, I just had to twist my hands together, over and over, like Lady Macbeth.

But I finally uttered a single, "No."

Steph gave me a sharp look. "He lives with Liam."

"I know," I said with a sigh. "I don't think Liam's in any danger. I don't even think *I'm* in any danger. I just... don't trust him. He won't meet my uncles. He avoided the Square entirely until he just *had* to see Cleopatra. And he was saying something to her that I only partly overheard."

"What's that?" Steph asked.

"He said 'if that's true, why didn't he tell me?' I don't know what truth he was referring to. He told me later they were talking about Barnardo, which would seem logical since we were asking questions about Barnardo."

"But you think he meant your father?" the Wizard asked.

I just nodded mutely.

"What do you think?" Steph asked the Wizard.

But when he answered, it was me he was speaking to. "I think you're right to trust your instincts. Maybe not when you called out to your father. I really wished you'd come to me with that plan first. But feeling like great forces are working all around you and there's no way to know who to trust? Trust that instinct."

"I will," I promised.

Which wasn't exactly a comfortable promise to make. It felt too much like agreeing to run and hide every time a cloud passed in front of the sun and a shadow fell on me. Could I live being that paranoid all the time?

And it certainly didn't help when Steph asked, "Should Tabitha come live in the Tower? I mean, stay here? Until it's safe?"

"What's safe?" I shot out before the Wizard could even open his mouth to respond.

But that got a chuckle out of the old man. "She's quite right," he said to his apprentice. "We could keep her here, and keep her safe. Maybe, for a time. But at what cost?"

"Just until we know what this Benvolio Ward is up to, and whether Mercutio is part of it or not?" Steph said.

"I don't think my brother is evil," I said. "I just don't think he's being straight with me."

"I don't think your father is evil either," Steph said. "Just ambitious in a way that's likely to leave you hurt."

"I don't think my brother is in league with him," I persisted.

"He's living with Liam right now precisely because he didn't want to get by just on the merits of the family name. Why would he do that if he was secretly plotting with our father?"

"It would certainly be helpful to get more of a sense of who your brother is and what he wants," the Wizard said. "At the very least, the one element we've been lacking in mastering your power is the other half of your symbiotic pair."

"She needs an order mage to master chaos?" Steph asked, but with the wonder-struck tone of someone who had just had an epiphany.

The Wizard just gave him a casual shrug. "If he can be trusted, we can bring him into the Tower, and perhaps then you can hone your control to the point where that bracelet becomes a thing of your past."

"But if he can't be trusted?" I asked, looking at the silver bracelet.

The Wizard didn't answer.

But the heavy sigh that escaped him was really answer enough.

CHAPTER
TWENTY-FOUR

As tired as I had felt sprawled out on that carpet in the library, I only seemed to get more tired after Steph had brought me home and my uncles had tucked me into bed. Houdini curled up with me, and we both slept through the night and halfway through the following day.

And even then, I still felt exhausted. It was like trying to recover from the worst flu of my life. I was tired and achy, and I knew I was cranky and ill-tempered.

It was a good thing my uncles were home and could run their bookshop without me. I wasn't any good for anything. I could barely get down any food, and then I'd be back in bed, sliding in and out of a restless doze.

Houdini never left my side. Not for three whole days.

Then, on the fourth day, I woke up, and it was like I was in a whole new world. The sun was more golden, the air cleaner, the warmth of the day perfectly comfortable without tipping into too much heat or humidity.

I went down to the kitchen, still in my pajamas, to find my uncle Frank making scrambled eggs in a cast-iron pan. The smell of butter and fluffy eggs made my stomach growl so loudly that Frank turned around with a laugh.

"I guess you've got your appetite back!" he said. "Grab a plate. You can have this batch."

"I can wait," I said, but he was already waving my objection aside before I'd even made it. I fetched a plate from the open cabinet and watched as he heaped great golden mounds of cooked egg on it. Then I carried it over to the dining nook and dug in.

Frank used cream in his scrambled eggs rather than milk, and there were flecks of minced fresh chives mixed in. I shoveled in forkful after forkful, only pausing to give him a quick thanks when he set a little plate with two slices of buttered multigrain toast in front of me.

"It's good to see you feeling better," he said, then went back to the stove to plate up his own eggs.

I was just using the crust from my toast to soak up the last of the buttery eggs from my plate when my uncle Carlo came into the kitchen.

"Ah. You're up," he said, giving me a soft smile. "You look better."

"I feel better," I said.

"Eggs?" Frank offered, half getting out of his side of the booth.

"No, just coffee for me," Carlo said.

Frank shrugged, then got back to work on his breakfast.

I watched Carlo as he moved around the kitchen, ostensibly getting himself a cup of coffee from the waiting carafe in the coffeemaker. But in the process, all the things that Frank had left in disarray while making breakfast just quietly arrayed themselves once more. The salt and pepper shakers lined themselves up on the back of the stove, the egg shells left resting on a paper towel found their way to the trash, and the extra utensils Frank had left out after digging out his favorite spatula returned to their proper places.

"Uncle Carlo, you're an order mage, aren't you?" I asked.

He looked up at me in mild surprise. Which only sold the point that he didn't need to be looking down at his hands pouring coffee into his favorite mug to know just when it was full and to stop pouring.

"That's not an academic track anymore. You know that, Tabitha," he said.

"But still," I said. "That's what you are."

He poured a little cream into his coffee, then returned the carton to its proper place in the icebox. Not where Frank had left it.

Then he came over to the booth. Frank had already slid over to make room for him. Carlo sat down, gave his husband a quick good morning kiss on the cheek, then took a preliminary sip from his too hot coffee before finally turning his attention back to me.

"In another era, that's what I would have been," he said. "It's not forbidden magic, but it's still something that's safer not being discussed out loud."

"In our own kitchen?" Frank asked, looking around the cozy little room.

Carlo just shrugged.

"My mother is your symbiotic partner," I said. "You're twins."

"Yes, just like you and your brother," he said. He took another sip of coffee, then said, "I suppose you're wondering if things would've been different, if you'd grown up together. And perhaps they would have. But it wasn't possible."

"Why wasn't it possible?" Frank asked.

It was actually handy having Frank there during this conversation. Both because he was a prosaic and understood these things even less than I did, and he was willing to ask all the questions. But also because, as Frank was Carlo's husband, Carlo was very strongly inclined not to keep secrets from him.

"My sister was trained in alchemy, but that wasn't her actual calling," Carlo said to Frank, turning in the booth to face him as he spoke. "Her real power is something we call chaos magic."

"Chaos, like *chaos*?" Frank asked with emphasis.

"The magical definition has some specificity we don't need to get into," Carlo said. "The short answer is, yes. Chaos like *chaos*."

"And I have it too," I told him.

"The fire," he said at once, nodding to himself.

"Right, the fire," I said. The night we'd met, I had told him the story of my disastrous job interview. It had been a raw and painfully new memory for me when I'd told him.

If I had gotten that job, I would never have come to the Square, and discovered the bookshop or met any of the people who had become the best friends of my life.

But that didn't make that little niggle of regret go away entirely. Working in the All-Planes Athenaeum still would be a dream come true.

"Should we be worried?" Frank asked. His tone was trying to convey his usual jocular humor, but the nervousness in his eyes was all too real.

"I'm good now," I said, and showed him the silver bracelet around my wrist. "This keeps me in check. I'm learning how to control myself, but until I do, I wear this. Even in the shower."

"That's not going to tarnish?" Frank asked.

"It's magic, dear," Carlo said, and adjusted the frames of his glasses before taking another sip of his coffee.

My reawakening to the world was pretty well timed, since that day was the day planned for Miss Snooty Cat's wake. I had gotten a text from Audrey about it, and had promised I would be there, even though at the point where I said so I was working extremely hard just to keep finding the letters to type into my phone to tell her.

I went back up to my room to find something appropriate to wear. Not that I had any idea what someone wore to a matagot's wake, or a cat's. I decided it was probably the same as with a human's wake, and chose something dressy and in dark colors.

And was thankful for the break in the weather all over again. I only had a little way to walk outside from the bookshop to the catacombs under the prosaic comic shop, but long pants and long sleeves of navy blue would've been miserable the week before.

Houdini hopped up onto the bed beside me as I was slipping on my shoes.

"I was wondering where you'd gotten to," I said.

"I was in the nook reading our book, but I didn't want to be late for the interment, so I'm here now," he said, and blinked at me. No dog of his size should be able to convey so much lordly condescension in a mere blink. But he did it.

"Did you learn anything from that book yet?" I asked.

"No, not yet," he said. "But it's very interesting all the same."

"We'll check it out together as soon as we have the time," I promised him.

"I know we will," he said. Then he suddenly flopped down like he was going to take a nap right then and there. Only he just rested his head on my knee. "I don't know how Miss Snooty Cat did what she did for Barnardo. It isn't something that matagots usually do. I know, the Wizard showed me everything he had in his books about matagots, and he agrees it's quite a mystery."

"I don't suppose we'll ever know, now that she's gone," I said.

But Houdini lifted his head to look up at me. "I only meant, I *wished* I knew. If anything should ever happen to you, I should wish to do the same. If only I knew how."

"Me, too, buddy, for you," I said, and scooped him up into my arms to nuzzle him.

My blouse was now covered in dog hair, but what did it matter? It was dark colored enough. Who was going to notice?

And, given how Barnardo had always been covered in Miss Snooty Cat's hair without really noticing, it just felt appropriate.

The two of us walked down to the Square, and without really having planned it, met Audrey and Liam just emerging from the teashop. Audrey ran over to give me a hug. I hugged her back, watching over her shoulder as Liam tried very hard not to look like he was stifling a yawn.

"It's kind of the middle of the night for you, isn't it?" I asked.

"I have tonight off, but yeah," he agreed. "Shift work is quite the experience."

"I'm sorry," I said. He raised a questioning eyebrow at me, and I went on. "I feel like it's my fault. Because of the spell."

"'Fault' isn't the word I would use," Liam said. "Tabitha, I'm really grateful you found this job for me. Tough as it is, I can make rent now. And I still have comic book money."

"I know," I said. "I just have this feeling, like because I tweaked the spell, it wasn't really doing anything for you. It was doing something for me."

"The dragon book?" Audrey guessed.

"The dragon book," I agreed.

"So it *was* useful?" Liam asked hopefully.

"Not yet, but I think it will be," I said. "But my point was, maybe you and Audrey should try the spell again. See if it brings another job opportunity into your life path."

"Something with more normal hours, maybe?" Audrey said.

"That *would* be nice," he said musingly. Then he shrugged. "Sure. What can it hurt?"

"And who knows? Maybe you'll find another strange artifact that's just the thing Tabitha never knew she needed," Audrey said.

She was joking, but I couldn't help flinching a little. The urge to hope he *could* find something else for me—something about chaos magic perhaps?—was just too strong.

But all of our laughter, nervous or otherwise, died away as we reached the steps down to Volumnia's abode. We picked our way down the moss-covered steps of stone worn treacherously smooth by centuries of footsteps. At the bottom, we found the heavy wooden door already standing open to receive us.

Barnardo was waiting for us there. He looked pale even in the dim light inside Volumnia's mud room, and so very fragile and thin. He hadn't gone shopping since being released for the hospital, clearly, as he was wearing his favorite white linen suit. It hung off him in folds, making him look like a little boy wearing his father's clothes.

"Thank you for coming," he said, hugging Audrey and then me and then finally Liam. "Thank you for everything."

"I'm sorry it took too long to save Miss Snooty Cat too," I said.

He didn't answer, just nodded, but I could tell by the way he suddenly clenched his jaw that it was only because he didn't trust himself to speak without bursting into tears.

Glancing at Audrey and Liam, I could see we all felt the same way.

It was almost a relief when Volumnia suddenly appeared among us. I usually found her an eerie, disturbing presence, with her intense blue eyes and skeletal body and long white hair. And the way she just popped in out of nowhere was so much worse than when Steph did it.

But she spared us all from trying to soldier on through more painful small talk.

"Are we ready?" she asked, her hands pressed together. Then she nodded as if we'd all just telepathically answered her at the same time, and turned and led the way down the natural tunnel through the stone that twisted around on a luminescent-mushroom-lined path to the catacombs proper.

Where Miss Snooty Cat laid, wrapped in linen inside a sarcophagus like a tiny Egyptian pharaoh.

The ceremony was a bit of a blur, even the part where Steph was suddenly there with me, his hand in my hand, as Liam and Barnardo carried the sarcophagus deeper into the catacombs, to the wall vault that belonged to the Daley family.

"She's with my father now," Barnardo said as Volumnia, with strength I never would've suspected she had, rolled the stone door closed, sealing up the vault until such time as Barnardo himself should pass.

I hoped that wouldn't be soon.

Then we all went up to Barnardo's apartment, where he had left more food out than the five of us could possibly eat. It was all waiting at the perfect temperature thanks to his magic serving set, the egg salad chilling in its bowl while the baked beans bubbled in their crock in a warm, desultory way.

Barnardo disappeared into his bedroom briefly, and the four of us plus Houdini sort of hovered uncertainly until he returned. He had changed out of the suit into a pair of tracksuit pants and a T-shirt I had never seen him wear before. It was still a little big on him, but not distractingly so.

"We should eat," he said, almost chiding us for not doing so already.

"It looks fantastic, of course," Audrey said.

"Dig in," Barnardo said.

But none of us made a move for the table. We just stayed as we were, sitting on the arms of sofas or leaning against the walls. Like we were all waiting for something.

"Listen, I should explain about what I do for a living," Barnardo said.

"You don't have to," I said at once, and Audrey was already nodding her agreement.

We both ignored Steph's hard looks. As the Wizard's apprentice, he had responsibilities that had to come before friendship. But Audrey and I didn't.

"No, I want to," Barnardo said. "I've already spoken to the Wizard about it, and I'm under official investigation, but the Wizard is sure it will all turn out all right in the end."

"That's good news," I said.

"I wasn't trying to hide anything from anyone. It just didn't feel like I was doing anything wrong. I was just helping out a friend," he said.

"What friend?" Audrey asked.

"An online friend," he said, and didn't quite blush. It was like I could feel him willing that response not to happen. I wished I had that skill. But perhaps a side effect of his near-death experience was just not feeling that kind of social shame anymore.

"Was it Mark Beetham?" Liam asked.

Audrey and I both turned to him with our mouths agape. Liam also lacked Barnardo's ability to will blushing not to happen, and he turned a deep scarlet. "Sorry. It was clear he wasn't a suspect, so there was no reason to bring him up. But I could see the two of you had formed a bond."

"Oh," I said, the word propelled out of me by a sudden flash of insight. "Mark Beetham. MacBeth?"

"Oh," Audrey echoed me as she too started putting the pieces together.

"Yes, that's where we got the name from," Barnardo agreed with a very short laugh. "It was my idea. All of the marketing was my idea. Mark had discovered a talent for crafting potions he couldn't even explain. I found him on a magic-curious forum I at that time only rarely frequented, but there was just something about him. Sweet but shy, earnest but a little too withdrawn for his own good."

"So you pushed him into business?" I asked, puzzled.

"Kind of?" Barnardo said. "I just helped him get started. I designed his website for him."

"And filed his taxes, and registered his business, and handled customer service," Liam added.

"Leaving Mark to focus on the only part of any of it he enjoyed. Crafting the actual goods," Barnardo said. "I didn't tell him anything about magic, though. Anything he did, he worked out on his own. I didn't even give him any hints. Not that I could. I'm not skilled in that sort of magic at all."

"He just spontaneously discovered magic?" Liam asked. He almost sounded jealous.

But Barnardo finally was tinging just a little pink in his cheeks. "Actually, that bits funny. His mother has been buying products from a mail order company for years. Perhaps you've heard of it?"

"Croft's Concoctions?" Audrey and I said at once, then traded a happy glance.

"Exactly," Barnardo said. "I knew Ursula Croft, at least online. We've never met in person. But I knew she was a con artist through and through. In the early days, she did put some low-level magics in her wares. But after she had her customers hooked, she no longer bothered. She gaslit all of them, insisting if the products no longer worked, the problem was the customer. Mark thought that was shady, but he wanted to help his mom. So he reverse engineered as many of Croft's Concoctions as he could get his hands on. Then, once he had the basic principles down, he just... carried on with new goods."

"I have a feeling the Wizard is going to be paying that man a call," Steph said mildly.

"Oh, he already told me that was going to happen. But he did let me tell Mark first. Mark is such an introvert," Barnardo said with palpable fondness.

We all shared a quiet moment of enjoying Barnardo basking in that fondness. Then, without anyone saying a word, the tone shifted to a more somber one again. At first I thought this was just normal for a wake, even if it was a wake for a matagot.

But Barnardo had something else on his mind.

"She hasn't said anything. Has she?" Barnardo asked. He was looking down at the cream-colored carpet, but we all knew who he meant.

"No," Steph said. "And she's already out of authority custody. She's under house arrest, in her family's home in Manhattan."

"Good riddance," Audrey said.

But Barnardo just nodded sadly.

"We solved the crime, but we didn't get you justice," I said. "I'm so sorry, Barnardo."

"Oh, Tabitha," he said, looking up at me with tear-filled eyes. "I know it was out of your control. It was out of all of our controls. People like the Manx family, to them, the rest of us are just pawns in their little games. I've always known that. I don't blame you in the slightest for anything. Miss Snooty Cat and I, we just owe you more thanks than we could ever repay for standing up to them as much as you did."

"Technically, I'm a Ward," I said. I don't know why it felt important to say that in that moment. Maybe I was afraid that he had forgotten. That if he had remembered, he'd be less grateful I had been involved at all.

But Barnardo just said, "I'm sorry, Tabitha, but I'm pretty sure that just means you're a bigger pawn. They'll play you all the harder, because you might score them a queen."

I didn't know how to respond to that. But it felt significant, the fact that he hadn't said I'd *become* a queen.

I'd be traded for one. Discarded.

It felt all too true.

But Liam broke the uncomfortable silence with a soft inhalation of breath. Then he turned bright red, as we all turned to look at him a little too quickly.

"Sorry, it's just, the sunbeam through the window just reflected off of something on that wall. It glimmered a little, caught my eye," he said. "I'm sure it's nothing."

"No, I think you're right," Steph said. He leaned over to look at a random spot on the apartment wall.

Only it wasn't a random spot, really. It was directly behind one of Miss Snooty Cat's various cat beds.

The most elaborate of all of her cat beds. There were stacks of cat-sized pillows and an array of catnip-stuffed little mice lined up like a toddler's stuffed animals.

Barnardo looked up at Steph and Liam like he wanted to stop whatever they were doing, but couldn't muster the energy to do so.

Then Steph took out his wand and whispered a word. There was a crunching sound as the wall fell away in crumbling bits of sheetrock.

And then the crunching became a tinkle. The tinkle of coins

against other coins. A waterfall of gold coins just came pouring out of that wall space.

There was a hefty pile when it slowed to a stop, but Liam was poking his head inside the wall space.

"It's not just this panel. It's all of them," he said. "I can see through knots in the two by fours. All the panels, all full of gold."

"But my father invested everything she gave him," Barnardo said. "I made the last deposit the morning he died. That was the end of their relationship."

"But the start of yours," Steph said. "I guess she thought the being caught by you first part was unnecessary."

"You always fed her very well," Audrey said.

"She stored a coin for every day she spent with you," I guessed.

And Barnardo finally broke down into tears.

CHAPTER

TWENTY-FIVE

It was another week before I finally saw my brother again. I knew he hadn't left town, because Liam had seen him—albeit briefly and sporadically—at their loft. I could only conclude that he was avoiding me.

And try not to go crazy speculating on the reasons why.

That, on top of trying not to go crazy worrying about what my father was up to, and if he really was planning on moving into my life, was a lot.

But I had the perfect distraction in that book Liam had found. Houdini and I spent every hour we could poring over the pages. We didn't know which sort of dragon he was yet, but we had a few ideas about how we could find out.

And even more thoughts on which kind we hoped he'd be.

"Come on, frost breath would be awesome," I said to him. "White dragon is totally the way to go. And so appropriate for Minnesota. It had to be why you were drawn here."

"We already know the Tower is why I was drawn here, thank you very much," Houdini said with a sniff. "*Not* the winter, I promise you.

Agatha would force me to wear little boots when I went outside in the snow. I *hated* it."

"I hate to break it to you, but I have those boots in a box under my bed," I told him. "If it gets as cold this winter as it did last winter, I'll be forcing you to wear them again. And a sweater and windbreaker too. But if you don't believe you need them, perhaps a trip or two out onto the icy ground in January will change your mind."

I had been flipping through the pages of my journal, the one I had started just to track the progress of our dragon research, so it took me a moment to notice that Houdini had stopped answering me.

I looked up to find him gone from his chair. Then I felt him pressed up against my ankle in full tremble mode.

I was just peeking into the darkness under the table to see what was the matter with him, when a voice called my attention to the far side of the nook, beyond the currently blank blackboard.

"I'm sorry to interrupt. Were you talking to your dog?" Mercutio asked as he stood there, arms crossed, looking at me like I was crazy.

"It's not weird. Lots of people talk to their dogs," I said.

"Do they all imagine the dogs are talking back?" he asked.

I flushed red, but not with embarrassment. Just how much of our conversation had he overheard? Far enough back for me to have said the word "dragon" out loud?

But he didn't seem bothered by my lack of answer, just dropped his arms and strode over to pull back a chair and drape himself into it.

Seriously, stage actors have less awareness of how their bodies move through space. It was like he knew just how to hit his marks without looking at them, and just how to convey casualness in a way that didn't feel remotely casual to me.

"I've been leaving you messages," I said to him, trying for a little casualness myself as I closed my journal, then the copy of the dragon book itself, and slid them both off the table and onto the seat of the chair beside me. Then I folded my hands on the tabletop, as if I had cleared the way just for that gesture.

He raised an eyebrow at my folded hands, but then said, "Yeah, sorry about that. I had some things I had to think through."

I wasted a moment trying to guess what those things might be, before giving up and just asking. "Such as?"

He looked around, as if to make sure no one in the bookshop was close enough to overhear. Although the magic of the bookshop kept that from happening.

Usually. Why *was* the bookshop giving him so many passes into my space?

But my brother was already talking. "I'm worried. About you. Well, no. I mean, *for* you."

"Why?" I asked.

He looked around again, then got up and moved to the chair closest to me. I was vaguely aware of Houdini sort of yelping in alarm before scurrying to the far end of the table. Not that he'd been in any danger of getting kicked.

All the affectation was gone from Mercutio as he sat down in that chair, then leaned over the arm to put his mouth closer to my ear.

"I think our father is coming," he said.

"Why do you think that?" I asked.

"I hear things," he said. "I know people, people you'd be happier not knowing, believe me."

"People who can lure someone like Antonio Talbot halfway around the world? And then convince him to set himself on fire? Just to keep me from getting my hands on an out-of-date astronomy text? Those kinds of people?" I asked.

He sat back enough to look me in the eye.

He looked genuinely shocked at my words. I wanted to compare it to the swagger he had used to walk up to my table and declare it sincere while the casual swagger had not been.

But wasn't that just what a really good actor would count on?

Putting on just enough of a show when it didn't matter that it didn't look like you were putting on a show when it did?

Only that wasn't really acting. Not for entertainment, anyway.

No, that was more like... spy craft.

"Tabitha?" he said.

"Why would anything our father did make you worry for me?" I asked him instead. "He might be a horrible human being, but he's still our father."

"He's ambitious," Mercutio said.

"But he stepped down from the one political position he had. Why would he do that if he was seeking a higher office?" I asked.

Mercutio actually laughed at that, which irritated me. It sounded too condescending by half.

"Sorry," he said. "It's just... that's not the kind of ambition I'm talking about."

"Aren't the Wards already filthy rich?" I asked. "I mean, there's always more money to be had, but somehow I don't think that's what you mean."

"No, I'm not talking about wealth either," he said.

"Then what?" I asked.

"You know what we are," he said, whispering close to my ear again.

"Yeah," I said, not sure where he was going with that.

"Did it ever occur to you that we were deliberately created?"

"Like a planned pregnancy?" I asked. "Or deliberately twins? Can that be done?"

"Of course it can be done," he said darkly. "We're more than twins, you know. You *know* you're not supposed to even exist."

"What are you saying?" I asked.

But he just stared at me. Kind of like how the Wizard does, when he's waiting for me to answer my own question.

"You're saying our father deliberately had children with our mother because he wanted an order/chaos pair of children?"

"Did you think it was a love match?" he asked almost tauntingly.

"To be honest, I hadn't thought much about it at all," I said.

Although, to be even more honest, yeah. I had. Who imagines their parents hooked up just to breed? And because they were a part of some conspiracy?

"So you must be worried about you too, then," I said. "Or you think you're powerful enough to take him?"

I had been trying for a joke, but his response was deadly serious. So much so he was squeezing my hand on the arm of my chair a little too tightly.

"I know I'm not," he said. "But I'm not the one he wants."

"You just said he made both of us," I reminded him.

"He needed to make an order/chaos pair because it's the only way to make a chaos magic wielder," he said.

He stared straight into my eyes, as if daring me to argue his point.

But arguing points was no longer top on my agenda.

Because something in his tone, in his eyes, in the expression on his face, was telling me something else. Something important.

"Mercutio, you don't think you're just some kind of... spare?" I asked.

"This isn't about me," he said, but I saw the hurt in his eyes all the same.

"You do. You think you were only born to create me, and now you're just extra. Is that why you've walked away from everything in your life? Did you just start thinking that when you came to find me?"

It fit. It fit so perfectly.

"Forget all that," he said, waving his hand as if he could just erase the point. "I just need you to know, I think you're in danger. Real danger. And it's only going to get worse when he actually gets here."

"So he *is* coming?" I said.

Not really a question. But I had kind of hoped he'd answer it, anyway.

But he just sat staring at the table as if there were a particularly engrossing book laying open there.

Then, for the second time in less than ten minutes, I nearly jumped out of my skin as a voice filled my nook.

"We're heading upstairs to dinner now, Tabitha. Frank is making Greek..."

But my uncle Carlo's voice trailed off as he came around the corner of the same aisle Mercutio had emerged from.

And caught his first sight of his nephew. My brother.

I had never seen him so emotionally struck in my life. At first I worried that the compulsion spell that kept him from talking to me about certain things about her had suddenly gone into overdrive. Could it throttle him to keep him from speaking?

But then he raised a trembling hand and adjusted the steel frame of his glasses.

"You're Mercutio," he said, his voice still thick with emotion. "You have to be. You're the spitting image of my sister."

"How long has it been since you've seen her?" Mercutio asked.

It sounded conversational enough.

But from the way Carlo sputtered, it was like he felt it was a test. One he was failing. Like even at his age, he still had anxiety left over from his schooldays strong enough to cripple him.

"It's been a while," he got out at last. "Too long. Come here, Mercutio. I would very much like to hug you. To be sure you're real."

"All right," Mercutio said, with his familiar mischievous smile falling into place. He pushed away from the table and sauntered over to Carlo. Mercutio had at least six inches on our uncle, and despite Carlo's girth through the stomach, his shoulders made him loom wider as well.

But then my brother bent and caught our uncle up in the biggest of bear hugs. Carlo quickly reciprocated, slapping Mercutio on his muscled back affectionately.

"Obviously, you're invited to dinner as well," Carlo said as he stepped back and adjusted his glasses again.

"I would love to," Mercutio said with a wide grin. "Greek, I take it?"

"Greek lamb and cabbage," Carlo said. "There's tomato paste involved as well. And feta cheese."

"It's awesome," I said, more to rescue Carlo from his nervous yammering than anything.

"Shall we?" Carlo asked.

"Lead the way," Mercutio said. Then he glanced over at me. "Coming?"

"Go ahead. I just need to get my dog," I said.

He shrugged and strolled after the still chatting Carlo.

I dropped to my knees and found Houdini at the far end of the table. He had stopped trembling, but his eyes were huge.

"Are you okay?" I asked him.

"I think he heard me," he said. Even in my mind, it sounded like he was whispering. "I think he heard me talking to you."

"He didn't seem to," I said.

But I couldn't be sure.

"Do you think he heard us talking about dragons, or only about winter?" Houdini asked.

"You didn't hear him approach, either?" I asked.

"No, and I *should* have. I *should* have," he said with bitter self-recrimination.

"He's a sneaky guy," I told Houdini as I scooped him up into my arms. "I really don't think he heard you. And if he did, he only heard us arguing about wearing boots in the winter."

"But how can you be sure?" Houdini asked.

I snuggled him closer to my chest as I made my way towards the central staircase, the one that would take us all the way up to the apartment on top of the bookshop. To the kitchen where lamb was surely already browning on the stove.

"Because the bookshop let him in," I said at last. "The bookshop let him in, not just in the store or up to the fourth floor, but into our nook. It wouldn't do that if he had bad intentions. And it wouldn't have let him near us when we were saying things it knows we want to keep secret."

"We can trust the bookshop?" Houdini said, and it was about half rhetorical question and half genuine inquiry.

"We can trust the bookshop," I assured him, and hugged him a little tighter.

"Okay, we'll trust the bookshop," he agreed. But then he put his head on my shoulder, nose close to my neck. "But I'm going to work harder to pay attention to where your brother is. Especially when he is close."

"I wouldn't object to that at all," I said.

Then we were in the kitchen, a tiny room that was somehow no more crowded with four humans and a dog in it than it had been when I had first arrived and it had just been three humans.

Like it expanded to fit us, if only a little.

Yes, the bookshop protected the Greene family. And watching my brother help Frank put the casserole dish full of chopped cabbage into the oven to brown, I knew Mercutio was a Greene too. He was part of our family, there in that kitchen.

More than that, as Frank turned his attention back to the lamb cooking on the stovetop, I saw Mercutio moving around him with his usual effortless grace. And in his wake, he left neatness. Spatters from the cast-iron pan disappeared from the counter beside the stove, the core and discarded outer leaves from the cabbage found their way to the trash, and the bottle of olive oil was recapped and put back in its proper place.

As if Mercutio just *knew* where its proper place was.

All of that had happened so quickly, like a reverse tornado, that no one but me even noticed it. But it was like a balm to the last of the worries in my soul. He might have inherited his looks from our mother, but he had inherited a lot of other Greene genes from our uncle Carlo as well.

And I knew I was right. The bookshop would never do anything that would put me in harm's way. So I snuggled Houdini tight, then slid into the booth across from my uncle Carlo, and prepared to do something I had so rarely done in my life.

To have dinner with my family. My ever-growing family. Perhaps some day soon my mother could be there with us too. But in the meantime, the four of us were family enough for me.

If the kitchen could expand to include my brother into our trusted family circle, my heart could too.

ABERGAVENNY'S CORNERSTORE
THE VIOLENTA COURT BOUTIQUE
BARTHOMEW BULLEN'S POTIONS & MAGICAL SUNDRIES
THE SQUARE PUB
THE WIZARD'S TOWER
LEBEAU'S FRENCH BAKERY
VOLUMNIA'S STAIRCASE
COMIC SHOP
PORTAL
THE BITTER BREW COFFEESHOP
VACANT STORE FRONT
INANNA SALON & SPA
THE WEAL & WOE BOOKSHOP
THE LOOSE LEAVES TEASHOP

CHECK OUT BOOK FIVE!

Tabitha Greene grew up all alone, shuttled from magical academy to magical academy with no rhyme or reason. She never stayed in the same place for more than a matter of weeks. Ever.

That all changed when she moved in with her uncles to help them run the Weal & Woe Bookshop in the Square, a hidden magical neighborhood in Minneapolis. Now her uncles make her breakfast to start every day, her neighbors greet her whenever she passes them, and she has friends who mean the world to her, and she to them. She even found a brother she never knew she had.

All that, and a little dog too. What's not to love about that life?

But all of that is threatened when the father she's never met moves into the Square and opens a business of his own. The Shop of Wonders, where the proprietor knows just what item every customer never knew they always needed. People flock to shop in his store.

But when one customer turns up dead after leaving the store, Tabitha can't help suspecting the last man to see her alive. Even if implicates her father.

No, scratch that. Especially if implicates her father.

The Novelty Shop Nightmare, Book 5 in the Weal & Woe Bookshop Witch Mystery series. Available August 13, 2024 direct from me at RatatoskrPressBooks.com or September 10, 2024 in stores everywhere.

THE WITCHES THREE COZY MYSTERIES

In case you missed it, check out Charm School, the first book in the complete Witches Three Cozy Mystery Series!

Amanda Clarke thinks of herself as perfectly ordinary in every way. Just a small-town girl who serves breakfast all day in a little diner nestled next to the highway, nothing but dairy farms for miles around. She fits in there.

But then an old woman she never met dies, and Amanda was named in her will. Now Amanda packs a bag and heads to the big city, to Miss Zenobia Weekes' Charm School for Exceptional Young Ladies. And it's not in just any neighborhood. No, she finds herself on Summit Avenue in St. Paul, a street lined with gorgeous old houses, the former homes of lumber barons, railroad millionaires, even the writer F. Scott Fitzgerald. Why, Amanda can practically hear the jazz music still playing across the decades.

Scratch that. The music really, literally, still plays in the backyard of the charm school. Because the house stretches across time itself. Without a witch to protect this tear in the fabric of the world, anything can spill over. Like music.

Or like murder.

Charm School, the first book in the complete Witches Three Cozy
Mystery Series!

THE VIKING WITCH COZY MYSTERIES

In case you missed it, check out Body at the Crossroads, the first book in the Viking Witch Cozy Mystery Series!

When her mother dies after a long illness, Ingrid Torfa must sell the family home to cover the medical bills. Her career as a book illustrator not yet exactly launched, Ingrid faces two options: live in her battered old Volkswagen, or go back to her mother's small town in northern Minnesota.

The small town that still haunts her dreams more than a decade since she last visited it. Or rather, not the town but the grandmother.

All of the drawings she fills notebooks with witches and the trolls that do their bidding? Not as whimsical in her nightmares as she sketches them in the bright light of day.

If not for her beloved cat Mjolner, living in the Volkswagen just might tempt her.

But the cat wants four walls and a door, so north she goes. And finds trouble in the form of a dead body before she even finds her grandmother's little town. How much can a town of stoic fishermen possibly be hiding?

As Ingrid is about to find out, quite a lot.

Body at the Crossroads, the first book in the Viking Witch Cozy Mystery Series!

ALSO FROM RATATOSKR PRESS

The Ritchie and Fitz Sci-Fi Murder Mysteries starts with Murder on the Intergalactic Railway.

For Murdina Ritchie, acceptance at the Oymyakon Foreign Service Academy means one last chance at her dream of becoming a diplomat for the Union of Free Worlds. For Shackleton Fitz IV, it represents his last chance not to fail out of military service entirely.

Strange that fate should throw them together now, among the last group of students admitted after the start of the semester. They had once shared the strongest of friendships. But that all ended a long time ago.

But when an insufferable but politically important woman turns up murdered, the two agree to put their differences aside and work together to solve the case.

Because the murderer might strike again. But more importantly, solving a murder would just have to impress the dour colonel who clearly thinks neither of them belong at his academy.

Murder on the Intergalactic Railway, the first book in the Ritchie and Fitz Sci-Fi Murder Mysteries, available everywhere books are sold.

FREE EBOOK!

Like exclusive, free content?

If you'd like to receive "A Collection of Witchy Prequels", a free collection of short story prequels to the Witches Three Cozy Mystery and Viking Witch Cozy Mystery series, as well as other free stories throughout the year, go to my website CateMartin.com to subscribe to my newsletter! This eBook is exclusively for newsletter subscribers and will never be sold in stores. Check it out!

ABOUT THE AUTHOR

Cate Martin has written stories which have appeared in the **Mystery, Crime and Mayhem** quarterly magazine as well as in the annual **Holiday Spectacular** Advent calendar of holiday stories. She is also the author of three witch mystery series: **The Witches Three Cozy Mysteries**, and **The Viking Witch Cozy Mysteries** and **The Weal & Woe Bookshop Witch Mysteries**. She currently lives in Minneapolis, Minnesota. You can learn more about her work at Cate-Martin.com.

ALSO BY CATE MARTIN

The Witches Three Cozy Mystery Series

Charm School

Work Like a Charm

Third Time is a Charm

Old World Charm

Charm his Pants Off

Charm Offensive

The Witches Three Cozy Mysteries Books 1-3

The Witches Three Cozy Mysteries Books 4-6

The Viking Witch Cozy Mystery Series

Body at the Crossroads

Death Under the Bridge

Murder on the Lake

Killing in the Village Commons

Bloodshed in the Forest

Corpse in the Mead Hall

Slaying on the Lake Shore

Bones by the Forest Road

Sacrifice Behind the Falls

Body Under the Café

Assassination in the Glade

Bewitchment After the Storm

Predator in the Lanes (available January 14, 2025 direct from me or February 11, 2025 in stores everywhere)

The Viking Witch Cozy Mysteries Books 1-3

The Viking Witch Cozy Mysteries Books 4-6

The Weal & Woe Bookshop Witch Mystery Series

The Teashop Terror

The Salon & Spa Scandal

The Bookseller Blunder

The Entrepreneur Enigma

The Novelty Shop Nightmare

The Courtyard Conundrum (available December 10, 2024 direct from me or January 14, 2025 in stores everywhere)

www.ingramcontent.com/pod-product-compliance
Lightning Source LLC
Chambersburg PA
CBHW061819190726
48289CB00007B/2250